T0023162

PARIAHS

Copyright© 2021 by Mbarek Ould Beyrouk
Translation copyright (c) 2023 by Marjolijn de Jager

PARIAS was first published by Sabine Wespieser Editeur
13 Rue de L'Abbe Gregoire, Paris VI © 2021

Manufactured in the United States
First Paperback Edition by Schaffner Press,
Tucson, Arizona

Cover design, illustration, and book interior illustrations by
Evan Johnston

All rights reserved.
Except for brief passages quoted for review, no part of this book may
be reproduced in any form without the permission of the
Publisher.

ISBN: 978-1-63964-005-8
Ebook: 978-1-639644-006-5

PARIAHS

BEYROUK

A NOVEL

TRANSLATED FROM THE FRENCH
BY MARJOLIJN DE JAGER

SCHAFFNER PRESS

CONTENTS

THE FATHER

You who are my Life,

I write to you through words, you know how well words manage to hide things. I write to you beyond the black screen that wants to separate us, this river of uproar and oblivion. I want to cross the boundaries of the unknown and go to you there in your dominion of light, where you await me in silence. I want to meet you beyond the realm of words.

You know very well, my darling, that I don't know how to talk, you know that my truths shriek inside me but don't know how to come together, complete each other, become sentences, speech. The essence of my life lies deep inside me and it's only when I shout or weep that strands emerge from the depths of my being. That's the moment of erupting truths, but also of faltering madness, you know those moments. I don't know how to talk. That's why I'm writing to you. But truth be told, I don't know how to write either, I only know how to mark white paper with black tears.

There is nothing around me, dear heart, there are no flaking walls on which wretchedness has transcribed its grief, there are no men lying on pallets, weary, woeful, waiting for an inaudible call from destiny, there are no horrible drains that let the nauseating odors from the courtyard come through, there are no sounds that crowd the air, often punctuated by screams, even the always so present Ali isn't here, wanting to be my friend and determined to cover my head with the fabric of his concern. No, here there's no one. There's only you who fills my mind and this immense building with your flawless presence.

Yet, they are untold in number. They fill the space with their grunts, they laugh, they yell, they sing, they weep, they loudly lay claim to life. They don't know that they're already dead. The others, those who see the sun rise, have affixed indelible marks on their foreheads, marks that they will bear forever, these stigmata are the signs of overall rejection, the hot iron on their conscience. The others will not see you anymore, will not listen to you anymore, they've written something on your destiny's logbook. And when they open that little book, your names will be there, clearly underlined, etched in the dark color of exclusion, and they will shake their head and look at you contemptuously, with pity for the best among them, and they'll say: 'Oh, no, sorry, you're already done for, erased from the list of those who are alive because those are the ones we see, you on the other hand... excuse us—next!'

For me, my darling, it's different: I am somewhere else, I do not lay claim to a future, I don't ask for a seat to attend the show, I no longer want a place among the living, I'm only with you, in your infinitude, in your absolute, in your cheeks, in your loins, in your eyes that are extinguished yet remain lighted inside me.

■ ■ ■

Diallo just offered me a glass of tea, he sat down beside me and handed it to me surreptitiously under his robe. Drinking tea is forbidden here, bringing in a hotplate is forbidden, lighting a fire, smoking, laughing too much—there are so many taboos here, but also so much laxity. Diallo can't do without his tea, he says it's his drug, he has a little camping stove, I don't know how he had it brought in, but the searches miss it every time. Diallo is the perfect man, never any fighting, never any loud shouting, friends with everyone, pious even, especially on Fridays, and he has a beautiful voice, too, he loves to sing very quietly, his fluid voice reminds me of empty nights, of utter solitude, like an evening at the top of a high dune when everything is silent; his voice also reminds me of you when you would bow your head and sing the *tebbrae*, the poetry of women in love that you liked so much. Every day Diallo says that he'll be set free the next morning, he can't stay in prison, his fiancée is waiting for him. Her name is Raki. And every day Diallo waits to be called and have them say: 'Diallo, you're free to go, Raki is here waiting for you.' But the call doesn't come, his name doesn't echo between the walls of our cells. 'Maybe they forgot about me just now but tomorrow they'll remember.' Because Diallo has no earthly awareness of having lapsed once upon a time, he doesn't do anything wrong, the only offense he commits is stealing a sheep once in a while, oh yes that, because he likes fresh meat, he can't buy any, but he can't do without it. 'Ah yes, that, I can't do without it.'

You see, darling, everyone has his own life with its implausibilities and its unpredictabilities. Where then does life actually begin? Not at birth. Not until the unpredictable, the implausible happen, when madness comes to inhabit each of us, the passion that belongs only to the individual, that's when he will be he, that's when he will truly exist. For me, my madness began...

Where does my madness begin and where does it end? No, it hasn't ended, not even after you. It has no beginning either because I was waiting for you. I knew there would be a knock on my door one day, I've always known that my life would be turned upside down, that the improbable would happen. You know, I'm not one of those who wait indefinitely for the day that resembles day, the night that resembles night, no, I'm not one of those who take the route that all the others take, happy in the crowd, glad not to be just one. When we used to come back from the well, I was the only one who'd take a path that no animals or men had trod before, I'd create my way at the risk of getting lost and perhaps die of thirst, but I would create my way. Where did the high road originate, the frenzied horse that swept both of us off? There is just one single moment, the first one, that I want to remember.

■ ■ ■

You were laughing out loud as you looked at me, I was blind, I was already blind, swinging my arms, closing my eyes, and letting out bewildered, already strained *ah's*. Outside you could heard the whistling of tear gas grenades and the screams of the demonstrators. Without knowing how, I'd rushed into the first open door, eyes closed, your mother heaved an entire bucket of water at my face, I was rubbing my eyes, and couldn't stop muttering the slogans I'd been shouting all day long, which were lodged in my throat. Then gradually the haze dispersed and I saw you, you were laughing, you said: 'He's struggling, he doesn't even know where he is and he insults the government', and then you burst out laughing again. My torn shirt, my disheveled hair, my tearing eyes didn't touch you, you just thought I was ridiculous. I was completely surprised to find myself in front of this beautiful young girl making fun of my distress and seeing something farcical where I couldn't imagine there being any. Outside the demonstrators kept shouting, the racket of the tear gas canisters still filling the air and dismayed, I made a motion to go back out, but your mother held me back: 'No, that demonstration of yours is done, you'll get arrested, stay here! Wait until it's over.' To tell the truth, I didn't want to go anymore, I just wanted to prove to you that I wasn't some fool or coward, I didn't want to ever leave you, I was riveted to those eyes that were mocking me, to that houri face lit up with laughter, and to that radiant body proclaiming youth.

Ah yes, we often looked back on that time together to pause at that moment, and every time you'd say that, at that instant, I actually meant nothing to you, that I looked like a hunted squirrel, with ears on the alert and red eyes, that I looked awful, with my clothes in tatters and my voice shaking. And, not to be outdone, I would tell a little lie and say: 'I saw a young girl laughing idiotically, a Harlequin in her hand, guffawing at a hunted man in pain, an unruly, pampered kid out of a bad book who, more than a stupid novel, needed her bottom spanked.' From then on both my woes and my joys bore your name.

■ ■ ■

My darling,

I forgive everything. Now as I remember them today, my sufferings at your side were pure delight, something I didn't know at the time because I didn't know anything, but as I contemplate the mirror of my life, I've come to understand that you were its sole reflection.

It seems that I will soon appear before them. They will interrogate me, I can already hear the judge's voice: 'Name, first name, profession', posturing that will go on forever, and I'll even have a lawyer, I refused to retain one but they have appointed one for me. Just to play the game. There must be several of us. So my lawyer will sing for me and the whole courtroom will caw while I, the accused, will be elsewhere. They won't know. They don't know anything. How could they know when they weren't us, when we'd gaze at the sky and take bets on the speed of the moon and the clouds? The roundness of the full moon would illuminate the earth, then suddenly find herself to be the prisoner of a mass of very brown clouds, kidnapped we used to say. How much time would it take the moon to free herself from the dark forces and send us her white smile again? We'd count on our fingers, I almost always beat you, I had experience with the sky. How could they know, they who want to judge us? They have never heard our laughter rise and wander among a jumble of clouds.

You know, my love, our meeting was a miracle. Every love is a miracle, that's true. Just think, since the human race began how many encounters, loves, follies, flukes, unprecedented circumstances haven't there been so that we'd be born here; just imagine that maybe there was one chance in a billion for me to enter your house at that very moment, imagine that you might have been ugly, or simply gone out to buy bread, or not be you, I may very well never have known you. 'You and your philosophy', you would say, 'more nonsense!', but all around us there are nothing but miracles and in my eyes you will always be the miracle of miracles.

Do you remember? We'd sit for hours on end talking about almost anything. We'd repeat endless anecdotes, exchange facts of everyday life. The important thing was for sounds to emerge, so our presence could erupt, be translated into gratuitous flaming words, the music of our hearts. Sometimes I wouldn't really listen to you, I'd watch you speak, I'd follow the movement of your lips and the quiver of your nose, I'd be waiting for the smile that would brighten your cheeks and the laugh I'd try to catch in the air, not let it escape, lock it inside a golden vase, buried in the ocean, in the belly of a sea monster who'd be my friend, my slave, and who would guard it forever, for eternity, for me, only for me.

Sometimes we'd walk together, we'd match our steps to the beating of our hearts, and we'd go and have tea at one of your girlfriends' homes, there would always be people, I'd listen to your chatter and be a little jealous, but we'd wink at each other surreptitiously and, supreme moment of bliss, we'd sometimes hold hands, quickly, discretely, without anyone seeing us.

Occasionally, more rarely, we'd go listen to music at some celebration where often we hadn't even been invited, and you'd grab the chance to dance, to whirl around and call me in—shy as I was—to get me into the round.

True, I was jealous and you watched yourself be alive and paid no attention to the agonies I endured. You already had too many friends, they'd make you laugh, while I would look away sullenly. As it was, I know you were relishing compliments from men in the street, sometimes you'd disappear for hours during the day and would respond to my worries and my distraught face: 'So, I can't go out?' I would try to hold you back by sketching a marvelous future for you.

Oh, I know, you repeated it often enough: all that time I was lying to you. Oh, I know, my wealthy parents, a future that seemed easy, holidays abroad, it was all a sham. I had merely created a world for you, telling you a fable so you'd be happy, forget the others, and your mother would appreciate me. I was afraid of myself, my dusty universe, my lackluster condition, I wanted to remove the monsters who were hovering over our bliss wanting to smother it, remove the hostile hearts and putrid bellies, I was afraid of the battlements inhabiting people's heads. I'm not a teller of tales, no, no, and besides I wasn't lying only to you, but to the others as well, to your mother, especially to your brother who could have rejected me, refused to let me have you, I was prepared to tell lies to have you, but also to cross the Sahara alone without any water, to cross the sea without any boat, to go up to the sky on the back of a djinn.

I knew perfectly well that we were walking down pathways paved with lies, that we were breathing a deceptively fragrant air; I knew that sooner or later the effect would shatter and I'd find myself naked, but I didn't dare break the rapture, I didn't dare dismiss the dream and go back to banalities and exile. It couldn't last, I knew that, too, but I closed my eyes and told myself that it was the moment alone that mattered, the taste of happiness alone that should be lapped up to the point of exhaustion, letting not a single drop escape. Tomorrow didn't exist, not yet, the moment was man's and the future was God's. And then I would repeat to myself: All these are lies, everything around us—us, others, beliefs, names, titles, stories, newspapers, governments. And then, too, I wanted to erase, forget the trivial, everything that was not you, and my childhood, which I'd never told you about! My childhood doesn't exist, it's happy, without any wrinkles. Still, I will describe it to you. You have to know, they don't know everything over there where you are. So listen!

You now know that I have no name, yes, no name, no wealth, not even any real land.

We were nomads, we'd travel over pristine sands to find pasture, we'd run after the occasional grass that would be gone, we'd walk behind clouds and rain. Slaves of time, but only of time. A large family. The entire camp was one family, not many, about a hundred people, but we felt we were many, we were the universe, we lived on the horizon. Sometimes we'd lightly touch the rest of the world in passing, rapidly, just for what was needed, tea, sugar, peanuts, clothing, barley, just the necessities. We were a little scornful of the rich placid city dwellers, we sometimes felt sorry for them, they're prisoners we'd say, solitary individuals always watchful like animals, ready to tear each other apart over an ounce of survival. We were a single multi-headed being, fabulous and smiling, we grazed together, together, we paused together to look at the sky, we grew thirsty together… we danced together when the rain came, and the beautiful expanses. I was happy because I had the world in my eyes and the entire universe around me. I knew none other, true, but it was enough for me, it filled me.

That was a time of wandering and a time of passion.

The time of wandering consisted of looking for life, water, and grass; my uncle led the march and we'd move to the rhythm of the sun and the animals, we followed the trail of clouds and winds, we never got lost, we knew where we were and where we were going, give or take a few kilometers, the Sahara's echoes had whispered in our ears, travelers, wanderers, strays, visiting guests, and the sky, our past excursions and the experiences of the elders, it had all spoken, we had listened to all of it, and my uncle said: we're leaving, we'll follow this road, and when night had fallen he'd show us the star that would guide us, the camels were quickly saddled, and our children's eyes were already gleaming with the thousand lights that the unknown promises.

When we stopped for a few months, a few weeks, a few days perhaps, we would recreate the world around us, drive the stakes of our tents into the sand, thereby biting the earth as if we'd stay there forever. Life rearranged itself again, oblivion quickly expunged the hardships of the journey, habits were renewed, idleness took over again, the adults would doze off, say their prayers, converse at length, play interminable games of checkers, sometimes gently die. Passions, too, would be reborn, love and poetry refreshed the cheeks of young girls, young men would boast about their courage or the delight in the words they invented, couples formed and would sometimes become undone, we children could run around in the grass, draw figures in the sand, or laugh at our Koran teachers.

My darling, shall I go on describing a world for you that you always wanted to ignore? You felt no affinity with those 'Bedouins', you thought they were strange and dirty, their sometimes brusque manners offended you, you didn't like receiving them at home, and when I'd meet one of them and open my arms to him, you'd say to me: 'You have to wash up before you come near me'. I'd protest and take the world as my witness: 'This is my sky, this is my life, this is me.' 'No,' you'd answer, 'if it were, you wouldn't have kept them hidden from me.' I had nothing else to say but I'd still grumble a little. Yes, I know, my lies are what made you despise my people, you didn't want to hear anything more, right from the start you'd rejected anything that had to do with my past, you used to say (it was your favorite expression): 'It makes no sense!' But now that you are far away, there where there can't be any lies, where the humming of the world comes through clearly, I think, I know, that you will listen to me.

I didn't know my mother, no, never, she died in childbirth. That was our fate: women often died while giving life. Children didn't always grow up, djinns sometimes abducted them when they were very young, especially if they were good-looking and intelligent, they'd select them to take them away to their blind kingdom. In any event, that's what they said. That's why our mothers were always hiding us under the wide swaths of their clothing at the risk of smothering us; they'd also give us weird hairdos so we'd look ugly: you had to deceive the djinns, they'd be so eager to take the most beautiful children away with them to their dark realm.

Djinns wanted nothing to do with me. So I grew up healthy and strong, surrounded by the love of the whole camp and the protective wing of my big brother. After all, I barely knew my father, just a shadow, a faraway voice, a beard, that's all. He died when I was six years old, I think (we didn't count years, it could be fatal for your destiny, it would attract the evil eye, it was challenging God's goodness). Still, I remember his death very well. We were departing in a caravan, it was right at the start of the summer, we were leaving the sandy areas to return to an oasis, Teyarett, I believe. In any case, that's where we often used to spend the months of drought. I wasn't even aware of his death throes, my brother didn't wake me until very late into the night to bid him farewell, pray over his body with the others. The men buried him and then at dawn we left again. He remained beneath the burning sand with just a few stones to mark his tomb. My father's death has no address, nothing, the sand must have covered everything, no tombstone anymore, just Amessaga, a vast zone from which he didn't rise. Those who can go to pray on the grave of their loved ones are lucky, me, I cannot, my parents have gone back to the sand, melted into the dunes of the Sahara. That is the fate of our people.

My darling, I hesitate to tell you more because I know that you don't like long stories, that family sagas hardly enthrall you, and that you abhor hearing talk of sadness and death. But since I lied, I must reveal my story to you.

It was my uncle and then my big brother who took charge of me. I never had anything to complain about. I didn't want for tenderness or education. All the women of the camp were my mother, all the men were my father.

I was a happy child, playing at goading the animals, fighting at the water well, pinching the behinds of little girls, and the Koran teacher never struck me because I was an orphan. I was enjoying my situation, I didn't really understand it but I sensed that I had an advantage over the others, I was everyone's son, but I was also well aware of the limits of my status.

I learned to read and write at the Koranic school, the camp's *madrassa*. Don't think of classes, desks, a blackboard, no, it was under a tent, the marabou's tent. We arrived at dawn and wrote on tablets of hard wood with a *calame*, a pen made of acacia wood, while he dictated the suras to be recited. For the youngest ones the letters of the alphabet were drawn; and all day long we'd loudly repeat the lessons. The teacher listened and from time to time would correct a bad pupil on the head with his long stick. Later, we recited the camp's only grammar book by heart, and also learned the poems of the *Jahiliya* the ancient 'suspended odes':

> *I invoked your name*
> *While the arrows drank from my body*
> *And the sharp steel was sucking my blood*
> *And I kissed the swords because they were ablaze*
> *Like the glow of your luminous smile.*

Remember these lines? I used to love singing Antar Ibn Chaddad right into your ear. Ah, you liked that, though you'd always say that I wasn't Antar, that I was neither a prince nor a poet, nor a great warrior and—you'd add, wide-eyed—that despite everything you had 'foolishly' chosen me, and the smile that would appear faintly on your lips outlined every exquisite pleasure for me.

I could have left it at that, quit Koranic school with suras in my heart and poems on my lips, continue to live my life, the life of my fathers: peripatetic, with gentle stops, quiet loves, risky encounters, marrying a cousin, oases in the summer, wide-open spaces the rest of the year, thirsting for rain. But my big brother made the surprising decision to send me to the city for my education. Nobody in the camp understood; I had already learned to read and write, I had recited the whole Koran, I knew the poems of the olden days and the rules of grammar; what else could I possibly learn, they wondered? All I was missing was life experience, they added: get to know nature and the animals better, get to know the tribe and its customs better, all things that time teaches very well. So what would I be doing at school? My big brother stood firm.

■ ■ ■

My darling,

I had to interrupt my story. Because I was summoned to the visiting room. It was my brother. I have nothing to say to him. The course I took was different from his. I chose to use words different from his. We no longer speak the same language. He looked at me and I lowered my head. I'm the deserter who has lost everything. The spoiled child who, trapped by shame and crime, has cut all ties with his people. I had nothing to say, but he did. He talked to me about the camp, the grass that's growing more sporadic, the enfeebled animals, the school that's been opened down there (a triumph for him), about the whole tribe, and then the children, our children, as if nothing had happened, as if life had picked up its thread again, as if the world hadn't fallen apart with you. I listened in silence. Yes, I know: my brother didn't come to our aid when we failed, he remained deaf to my appeals, all he said was: 'You made your bed against my wishes, you'll have to lie in it', words that condemned us to suffering. I was punished for having loved you, for having followed you. But that was my brother's nature, I never held it against him.

He has changed, you know, my brother, the years of nomadic wandering have left furrows on his face and there's something like a crack in his voice now, a hesitance it seems, he's not sure of himself now, I sense it. He chose his own way, of course, but he doesn't know all its twists and turns, he no longer knows the secret of the sands, ah, the desert doesn't easily forgive those who forsake it, it stays clear of them for a long time, and they have to spend years to recapture its lost compassion. I don't look for compassion from anything or anyone, only from you, even now...

My brother went to see our children. He removed our son from PK7 and the perils of the street. He's taken him to our tents at the camp. He will better learn the things life's made of there. Still, my friend Moud and his wife really loved him, but how could they take care of their own offspring when the demands of life and survival force them to be outside every moment of the day and they themselves have no education whatsoever? In their environment children quite naturally grow up on the street. Our son will make a different life for himself, or at least I hope he will.

My brother wasn't able to see Malika, your brother wouldn't let him; he refuses any contact with my family, he broadcasts everywhere that I'm a murderer, that I put a spell on his sister, that our son was born out of wedlock, that he brings bad luck, that he doesn't recognize him as a nephew and that, since you're gone and I'm unfit, Malika now belongs to him, only to him. He's crazy, I swear. He's controlled by hate, he thinks he has values but his hands and his mind are empty, he has allowed a vacuum to occupy his entire being, to serve him as intelligence and guide. Malika won't be happy with him. My brother will certainly try to get her back later on, but I know that'll be an arduous task. Your brother, my darling, is a disaster.

No, I shouldn't invite you into the grim labyrinth of our darkness, no, you have reached the virginity that erases and recreates. And yet, yes, I have to tell you.

Ah, yes, I was at the point where my brother had that outlandish idea of sending me to school. My uncle had his own opinion on the subject: he said that today's school certainly trained the young, they were learning foreign languages and forgetting the language of their fathers, they were learning how to disrespect those close to them and disparage their culture, learning irreligiousness and the lies of these times, idleness and laziness, yes, he concluded looking contemptuous, they sure learn many things that we only sometimes encounter here, but which school there manages to increase tenfold.

My brother told anyone who would listen that the tribe really needed someone who'd be familiar with the realities of the time. The world had changed, he explained, the desert was being vacated. Enticed by the city's lights, people were departing every day, joining the new legions of heartless city dwellers. 'They're eating us little by little, those who're ravenous for the new times,' he added, 'and we really must defend ourselves, learn the secrets that will enable us to settle down and believe we're happy.'

Actually, my brother was afraid, he saw the world explode, saw the animals grow weak and their udders dry up, saw the bottom of the wells grow deeper, and he wanted to salvage our world, turn our life into a choice, yes, a choice. Later, he explained to me that he didn't want to be a Bedouin by necessity but by virtue, yes, that's what he said, honestly, that's what he said. He's an idealist, my brother.

But I hear something. It's the gong they sound to tell us it's time for bed, soon it will be lights out, and darkness will engulf our cells and the courtyard. The worst of crimes can be committed here, and they know it, they know that smuggling thrives here, that sharp knives appear by the light of flickering flames, that the strongest rule, the weak grow even weaker, that's pretty much the life, the true life to be reborn from the ashes of a brightness misguidedly adorned by fake daylight. But don't worry, my soul, I'm not afraid, I . . .

THE SON

It costs too much to love. I heard that once in a TV series and it's stayed with me. It's true, it's too hard to love, when I think of what happened, when the images appear in front of my eyes, the images of Papa, Mama, and little Malika, it hurts too much, I feel something tightening here inside and I feel like crying, then like rushing to the toilet but I don't, I stay, I hold it all in, it's just my stomach talking, and I say: I'm a man, real men don't cry, real men are tough. But, frankly, all of that stays right here, in my throat. And then there's PK7, there's Father Moud and Mother Maria, there's Sara, there's Momo, and Tenn and Selma. I just have to forget, not think a lot: it hurts too much.

With Momo I can forget a little. Momo has broad shoulders like an adult, and very large biceps, and his feet—you should see them – big and chafed, you'd think they cause him pain, but no, it's just the way it is because of walking barefoot in the mud and on the hot sand, that's how they came to be this way; and his back is very straight, like a big stick, and he even has a bit of a mustache, ah yes, just a tiny bit, he's almost a man. He's my brother, Momo is. My brother, not of the same father or the same mother, but he is my brother, he protects me, and besides, I live with him, and what I call his father and mother is

Father and Mother, that's the way it is, and he also loves me a lot, that's for sure. He's the real thing. When I grow up, I'll be just like him.

I have many friends, there's Massou who's always grumbling, it's his father who has the cart and who's strong while Massou cries over nothing, still he's nice; there's Milou who has no father, so everybody says, but he constantly repeats: 'My father... something or other', but we've never seen him; his mother does women's hair in her little shop over there; there's Sidi who stutters, he's the son of the muezzin, Sidi knows nothing except how to run, but in that he's really fast; there's Chik, they call him Toothless, he has no front teeth, his father left one day, his mother sells fritters at the market, sometimes he brings us a few; there's Saidou, his father sells bread and his mother is a seamstress, they have television at their house; and then there's Mokhis, Pele, Mino, Bahim, Papis and a few others, that's the PK7 sector, here we're all brothers even if we do fight sometimes. Momo is our leader, he's the oldest, he teaches us how to be tough, how not to back down.

Ah yes, with Momo you don't have any choice, you don't back down, you have to fight when you have to fight. Face to face with Saidou I was really scared, he has a big gut, he's always drinking Coke, his father sells bread, he has something here on his arms as well, maybe a talisman, I don't know. Saidou called me a 'son of a ...'. Momo didn't even look at me, he simply pointed at him like this with his finger. 'Crack his face!' he told me; so I had to go ahead and Saidou, quite pleased that it wasn't Momo, hurled himself at me, I got a lot of wallops all over everywhere, it hurt a lot, I backed off, I almost fled but no; because Momo's beating would be even worse, so I got up every time I fell, and finally I was able to bang my head really hard into Saidou's big belly and he fell down, he screamed, and I didn't give him any time, I whacked him with my feet all over his body, on his head, belly, butt, even his pecker, and he cried and cried until Momo told me to stop. 'That's how it's done, don't back off.' He's a tough one, Momo is.

But the real battle is with the kids from PK8. They're on the other side of the highway, where even the blacktop is bad, and trashcans between us. The kids from PK8 are our enemies, that's for sure, they smell bad because their fathers work with garbage and their mothers sell fish, and all the girls there are slu…, in any case that's what we all say here.

Momo always directs the brawl when we tackle the kids from PK8; he's up front with his slingshot and aims at them as if they were rabbits, he insults them, and we heave stones at them, we never back off. Once when we attacked them by surprise they fled toward the asphalt where they were almost crushed by the cars, so we pursued them some more, well, the others did, I stayed behind because my feet were sore.

Another time we just fought one on one, Momo knocked down their leader Merzoug, that was his name, we shouted really loud, and then left without any further ado; we went back to our district singing and dancing. Just as with playing soccer, we never finished a single match with those PK8 bastards, except maybe once or twice; it's always they who scream 'goal!' while we yell 'off-side!' The referee always comes from PK12, he's scared, too bad, we fight, sometimes kids get hurt and their parents take them to the clinic and then to the police station, while we stay put at home, on days like that we don't even go to the Play, and the next day, too, we let it go by, that's the way it is.

At the Play we all sit together on benches, by ourselves, as Momo's team we go first, Momo, then the rest of us; the others wait, that's the way it is, because Momo's team is Momo's team, it's not every kid in PK7, no. We're always in front, we play first. But when there's a match, Django, the owner, turns on the big TV and that costs more, but he gives credit, so we're almost always all there, we look around to see the faces, we're the Real, the Barça just have to behave, shush, we're the strongest in the neighborhood, when our team makes a goal we explode, very loud and strong, while they're only allowed to yell a little. Except when there's a *Clasico* match, that's serious business, those who aren't with the Real can just go somewhere else, even Django is with us.

The kids from PK8 never come here, it's taboo. And yet they don't have a Play where they are, closed down by the police, but they don't dare come here. Django, the owner, would actually like it but he knows: as soon as they come there's fighting, then the police.

In the evening after the Play, we often stay out, in front of the shop of Meimoune-who-sells-anything, and we tell stories, always films playing in our head, and very tough people who're fantastic, not like the stories Mama used to tell me, about the king's daughter, Ali Baba and so on, no, here it's really daunting, they're tough. Sometimes the kids fight, too, but not always. When they tell stories, I always doze off toward the end and Momo tells me to go home, but I stay anyway. Sometimes Momo takes me home on his back. In the morning, I can't remember anything, honest.

Sometimes it's Demba-the-madman who comes to tell stories and then the kids really have a good laugh.

Every kid in the neighborhood has a pocketknife or a real knife, I have just a small one hidden in my underpants, which Momo gave me. 'If anyone hurts you too much, shove it in his belly.' I know it's not good, Mama would never allow me to have something like that, she also wouldn't let me go to the Play or leave school. But Mama's gone and I'm all alone, and besides, as Momo says, you need to know how to command respect.

Once the police came, lots of them, they picked up a lot of kids and shut down the Play; a boy got himself killed over in PK10, it seems, a knife in his gut, but it's always the same story: the police shut down the Play and two days later it's open again. 'Django, the owner, pays off the cops, they're all corrupt.' And then Momo explains to me what corrupt means: it's someone who receives plenty of money without doing anything. 'Later on,' I said, 'I'll be a big crook,' and Momo just laughed, I don't know why.

Every so often there's an important match at the stadium which is far, very far, but we all go there, we have to walk a long way, it doesn't matter, sometimes we hook onto a car, one or two and even three of us, but no more, the driver doesn't see anything, so we're good, taxi free-of-charge, we wave when we pass our friends and when the car turns or stops, we jump, it's not always easy, sometimes we fall, fat Saidou always falls, he doesn't die. 'Immortal' we tell him, but I know: when I jump, I keep running a little longer, that's how you avoid coming down too hard. At the stadium we always root for Ksar, there's no important team at PK7, so we're for Ksar, they're the bosses over there, we jump up and down, we scream, we whistle, we dance on the bleachers, it's a lot of fun, sometimes a gentleman in a huge boubou hands out coins to us, so we scream louder, it doesn't happen every day but it's cool. Every so often it turns into a fight because those PK8 bastards always support Concorde.

Sometimes Momo takes us to the main market over there, it's far away, next to the grand avenues, you can even see the house of the President-on-the-photograph, and there's lots of beautiful houses, buildings, the police, the radio station, all those things, and then stores where they have everything, but we go to the center of the market, there's lots of people, lots of things, lots of stuff going on, lots of it, and more than anything it's full of women with bags crammed with money. We mustn't let each other out of sight and we have to be alert, at the slightest signal we bolt, the first one to pinch anything has to run fast and whistle; me, I never take anything, I'm with my friends, that's all, but when they whistle I run, of course I run, they've never caught me, we run all the way to PK6, the large space behind the factory, and they show what they have; often they have money, sometimes it's jewelry, sometimes nothing, we divide it, my share goes to Momo. Every so often a merchant or passer-by catches one of us, it's always someone who hasn't stolen anything, he opens his hands, nothing, he empties his pockets, nothing, he takes off his pants, nothing, his shirt, nothing, the cops come and slap him around a bit, haul him off to the station for a day or close to it, sometimes they take him back to his parents, but he never says anything because in our PK7 they're all tough, not like in other places.

At the Clinic junction it's more complicated, the kids from the Beyda district are there, you shouldn't go there by day, they're all there, you don't always see them but they're there, they steal, they sell a lot of stuff, things they stole; there are lots of taxis, lots of cars, lots of shops, lots of everything, and they, the Beyda kids, are in the middle of it all, and then, it's unbelievable, they sometimes have cops with them and shopkeepers, they're not just anybody those Beyda kids. So when we come, we just pretend to be passing through; if we steal, we steal only a little, and fast, and we leave, shouldn't stay, if those Beyda kids see you they take everything you have, then they beat you up and take you to the police and say: 'He's a thief', and the cops beat you up, too. And even the bus over there, we take it only when we have a ticket because the Beyda kids won't let anyone get on for free, just themselves and that's alright with the driver.

When we steal a cell phone or something it's always Momo who goes to sell it at the 'hot spot', the market for telephones and such, it's also full of crooks and even the kids from PK8 go there, but we don't fight when we're there, we say nothing. Sometimes I go there with Momo, I stay right behind him so I won't get lost. 'There are many, many people and all of them are crooks, they wear turbans, they smile, but they're crooks, they show you something: 'It doesn't cost much', but you shouldn't buy it, it's just rubbish.' Me, I don't talk to anybody, I stay right behind Momo, 'cause he knows where he's going, he talks to no one, he goes to his buyer, only his buyer, an old man with a white beard who examines the thing, then gives him the price; Momo's never happy but he always takes the money. 'That old man's a thief.' Sometimes, when it's really urgent, he sells things to Meimoune-who-sells-anything, but only when it's very urgent because Meimoune-who-sells-everything really doesn't pay anything.

Meimoune-who-sells-anything is the great shopkeeper of our district; he always gives us a little credit, a candy, a loaf of bread, cookies, and we pay when we can, but he isn't straight with us, Meimoune-who-sells-anything; when you're interested, he gives you a price: 'Fine, that's one coin', but later when you want to pay it's always two coins! That's how he is, Meimoune-who-sells-anything, and even the fathers say that he always ups the bill at the end of the month. He writes down what's owed and then he increases it; and when people protest, he replies: 'That's what it is, I wrote it down, look, can you read? No? So?', and then he gets angry. In the end, they pay, but he does always give credit, that's why people buy from him.

One-eyed Dahi, he doesn't give any credit, the only thing he knows is money, he gives nothing, he reads his book in his shop, he says nothing, just the price! When someone reacts: 'That's expensive' or 'You need to give credit just until tomorrow', he goes back to his book, reads out loud with his one eye, he's heard nothing, he doesn't joke, not even with us kids, he has no pity; when the ball lands in his shop, he takes it and slashes it, that's it, all you can do is cry over it if you want; and besides he's big and strong, always in a dirty boubou without any shirt and you can see his fat belly and even the breasts.

At the house there are many of us, there's Father, Mother, Momo and the children, me I don't exist, I'm excess because Father Moud isn't my real father and Mother Maria isn't my real mother, my real parents are far away, in heaven and in prison, I'm just an outsider, but I'm really comfortable, I'm fine here. When Salem, Papa's brother, came, right after 'it', to take me far away to the boondocks out there, I went at first but then, when I came back, I didn't leave again. I fled, they didn't see me for two whole days. Momo hid me, so then my uncle got tired, went back to his desert, which is where I didn't want to go anymore, it's too barren, nobody there, no television, no soccer, no buddies, no streets, no people, just camels and dunes, that's it. I'll tell you about it. And Mariem, the wife of my uncle-my-father's-brother, would never stop ordering me around, send me to the well, make me carry heavy loads, and very early in the morning wake me up to pray, I didn't like it, and besides, she sometimes said bad things about Mama, I didn't like that either; I'll tell you later.

It's fine here at the PK7, after all there's Momo who protects me, I follow him everywhere, he keeps me from thinking too much and from hurting all the time. Father Moud really likes me a lot, too, he's the one who took me in the night when 'it' happened, I was on the street, crying, all by myself because the police had cleared the place and everyone had left, so he kissed me and carried me in his arms, he knew Papa very well and Mama also, a little. Mother Maria said, 'We've enough mouths to feed here already', then she stopped talking because Father Moud doesn't say very much but when he does, truth be told, you don't argue with him, so I got to stay.

True, Father Moud doesn't say very much, still, when he has some money, he grabs my hand and takes me to the store to buy me candy or buttered bread, he also says nice things to me and prays for my parents every day. Mother Maria doesn't curse at me as she does her own children, she just doesn't talk to me, I can come and go as I please, like Momo who's almost a grown-up; true, she doesn't have a lot of time, she spends all day preparing the pancakes she sells at night, sitting down there in the main street. But she doesn't complain, her pancakes are famous, people even come from very far-off well-to-do districts to buy them, so thanks to her we're almost never hungry because even those she doesn't sell can be eaten, we mix powdered milk, water, and sugar and it's good. Except when it's repeated several days in a row. Father is a dockworker at the port, he doesn't always have work, but you can tell when he does, then he smiles and gives us coins.

No, I didn't want to leave, all my friends are here, and soccer, the Play, the streets I know, even our house, with nobody in it, it's locked, the door is old and tired, it's weeping, our old door, black with grime, the wood's coming off and kids pee in front of it, but it's still our house, I pass by it every day and kiss it lightly, not touching it very much, ah yes, that's where we used to live before, me, Mama, Papa and little Malika, that's where we were, we'd have our cereal in the morning, and I would go out to buy bread because Mama got up late and Papa was almost always absent, he worked up north in the mines, but we were fine, honest, even I wasn't the way I am now, I even went to school, well, I don't want to think about it too much, it's too awful.

I always wait to see Sara go by in the evening, she has a beautiful face and a sweet smile, she's not very old, older than me of course, but not very old, she wears very tight pants and sometimes she wears *pagnes* that firmly hug her attractive body, it's like a dune that body, and her eyes are like a window, I shouldn't say that, true, but I still think it. Sara works for people in the neighborhood, I don't know them very well, their children are too little, but the father has a car that makes a lot of noise and the mother actually sells vegetables down at the big market. When she passes Sara always smiles at me and sometimes gives me a coin, I'm embarrassed to take it, but I do so she won't get angry, I help her carry the basket she always has, with her bag, it's warm inside, it's the meal she brings home, where Sara lives, I don't know. She stops on the sidewalk and waits for the bus, you have to wait for a bus for a long time where we are, but I'm happy to stay with her, she sings melodies very softly and looks at me and smiles, she also talks to passers-by and then they laugh together, which I don't like. But afterwards I come back very happy. Momo doesn't like Sara very much. 'She's full of herself.' 'Why full of herself?' I ask but he doesn't answer.

Every so often I really wanted to go back to school, it was always dark there and you were protected from the sun, and there were so many students that the teacher couldn't say anything and we could just have fun, and during recess we'd play all sorts of games, except that the oldest kids used to rough us up a little but that's not so terrible, it's normal, besides I always had clean clothes, and my notebooks were neat, too, well almost. Only, since 'it' happened I can't go there anymore, the kids are just too mean.

Often we'd take on the *talibé* children, they live with the marabouts, they have no parents and come from somewhere far away, they're beggars and thieves and don't defend themselves, they put their arms over their eyes and cry, so we don't hit them too much, but they're idiots these *talibés*, they say they study the Koran and all that but they're hooligans, they 'get fried', take pieces of fabric and shove them into the mufflers of cars, then inhale deeply, it's rough, really, you see stars and hurt all over, me I did it once, I almost died, water even came out from you know where, and Momo told all of us 'It's illegal', but the talibés, they do it anyway and that's why we beat them, take their money and their rice, they're scoundrels those talibés.

We really have a good laugh when we see volunteers who say: 'We're here for the street kids, we're here to educate them. We set the right example, we help.' So then we play at being poor, really poor, we let them think we have no clothes, no food, that we get beaten and all that, some of the women among them even start crying, stupid fools! Sometimes they give us clothes, cookies, or knick-knacks, never any bills, but it's still good. Once we're gone, we make fun of them, they're so dumb those people, they know nothing about anything. Even so, there are kids who stay with them, live, work, and eat with them, like their slaves, we say.

Sometimes we go in the cart, it's a good day when we have the cart, it's Massou's father who lets him have it: 'Go on! I'm tired today', so then Massou calls us, just Momo and me, and we have a really good time. Momo takes the rope and stands up in the cart, crying 'Arr! Arr!', Massou and I hit the donkey with a stick and he hauls us off at a gallop, it's like being in a car, we have a good time and we use our hands as flashers when we turn and we yell 'Beep, beep' to alert folks, we laugh a lot. But we have to work, that's why we have the cart.

So we go to the market and Massou sees his father's customers, they always have things that need to be transported, sometimes far away, merchandise, sacks of rice, flour, other products we don't even know, and one time it was cookies, packs and packs of cookies, we ate so many that we all had a stomachache that night.

No one ever asks us anything at home, the mother is busy with her trade all day long, she's bent over the cooking pot, she stirs the dough, it's not a pretty picture over the fire, there's too much smoke because of the charcoal but it's always good afterwards, even the marabou comes sometimes, mumbles things, then he tosses a little of his saliva in the pot as a blessing, she gives him a few coins, that's why she often sells all of her cakes; the kids can cry all they want, she stays there, watching her huge pot, except when it gets to be too much for her, then she hands out a couple of smacks here, there, but that's it. Father Moud, when he's there, says nothing, especially when he's working at the port, he wants quiet, he sleeps, he hits whoever talks loudly, except for me, he just looks at me and tells me 'Ssshhh!'

There are many kids at the house, there's one who's nursing, he has only one tooth but he laughs all the time; there's a little girl, Selma, three years old, very small, who never cries, we can push her around, Momo and I, slap her cheek, she doesn't cry, that she doesn't cry makes us laugh and we always bring her candy because she's very cute as well, she calls us 'Ichi' and 'Ichou', we don't know why; there's Tenn, poor kid, he doesn't walk and his legs are super scrawny; then there's Toto, as they call him, he makes us laugh, too, he never learns anything at school, he dances like Michael Jackson; and then there's a baby in Mother Maria's belly.

Momo and I don't like staying at home very much, we're outside all the time, and when we come home late at night, we go to sleep in the little courtyard filled with charcoal waste and smelling like urine, Father Moud sleeps under a small tent to the side. When he snores really loud it means he's found work that day, which is good, Mother Maria and the little ones sleep in the only bedroom, I never go in there, it smells even worse than the courtyard.

I like it when we take the law in our own hands at night. There are men who come down here, they're dogs, they have beautiful cars and they come to 'spoil' the girls in the neighborhood, they give them money and then take them far away somewhere, and there's always one who comes back with a big belly, her parents weep, but there's nothing we can do, she's 'spoiled' Momo explains, no more husband for her, unless it's a jerk, a real jerk. So when those bastards come, we attack them with stones, break their windows, and they get away as fast as they can, unless they're smart, then they toss coins at us, we stop for a moment, but they have to move fast.

Momo sometimes takes the headlights from cars, he arrives quietly at night with a screwdriver or something like that, he leaves the car totally one-eyed, Mokhis is always with him to stand watch so no one will come, I stay far away, I wait; one time I saw them running, running, I didn't move, I was really scared, and then a man in a djellaba came by, the one who watches the cars I think, and he was shouting 'Thieves! Thieves!', he was chasing them, but they were faster, and then the guy came back, panting, he saw me and stopped, I was shaking, I was just going to tell him: 'It wasn't me, I didn't do anything!' but he yelled at me: 'What are you doing here at this hour, go home, one day you'll be a thief just like them, go home, you little good-for-nothing!' so I ran really fast.

Momo sells the headlights at PK10, where somebody buys them from him, he returns with many bills and pays for the Play for everyone and cakes for everyone as well, and he brings fruit for Selma and the children, he says they're vitamins and there's never any of that at the house.

Toto learns nothing at school, he has ringworm on his head but he dances, oh yeah, he really knows how to dance, Toto does, and it makes everyone laugh because he mimics Michael Jackson, always in front of the house, and people stop all the time, you see, he's very small and he turns and turns with his hand on his head, like Michael, so his hat won't fall off, although Toto, he doesn't have a hat, he just has ringworm on his head. He's sweet, except when he's hungry, then he opens his mouth wide and screams.

Tenn, poor kid, doesn't move, his feet are tiny and he drags himself along on his butt, and it makes Selma laugh when her parents are not around; because Father Moud and Mother Maria say that you're not allowed to laugh about Tenn: 'He's something God given, you shouldn't laugh, God doesn't like that'. But Tenn's always making faces and he imitates goats, so all of us, we can't help laughing, he's so funny, Tenn; sometimes he goes out and sits in front of the house under the tree and passersby give him some money, he takes it and laughs, doesn't even know what money is, but he takes it and laughs, Tenn does, and at times we even pick up lots of coins, then Momo takes some, I do, too, and the rest is for Mother Maria. Occasionally, Momo asks him to come sit under the tree and we wait until we have enough for the Play and some cake. When he feels like it, Toto plays Michael Jackson while Tenn grimaces and waddles, then suddenly people give more; we call it 'the big fix'.

But one day Father Moud saw it and got angry, really angry I tell you, he shouted, started breaking everything he could and yelled: 'We're not beggars, we're not beggars!' and for a long time afterwards he didn't talk to Mother Maria and warned that if Tenn went out begging one more time, he'd leave us forever, we wouldn't see him again and that really scared me, oh yeah, I was shaking, I swear, because when Father Moud says something he always does it. But Selma couldn't care less, she keeps asking Tenn: 'Why don't you go outside?' she's simply hoping for candy, but we, we stop her: 'Never, never, never you hear? Never again!' and then she does something with her mouth, with her upper teeth on her lips, it makes me laugh. But then we have to bring her to the TV, otherwise Selma will cry for a really long time. We don't have TV but we do have nice neighbors, Saidou's parents. We can watch TV in the courtyard whenever we want and sometimes me and Momo even leave Selma there and we go to the Play because that television has nothing on, no action movies, no wrestling, no cowboy and Indian films, no pretty women, nothing, just the President-on-the-photograph or talking heads.

Me, I'm somewhere near my little sister Malika every day. It's my uncle-my-mother's-brother who's taken her and he doesn't want to see me, never ever, he vowed, just her, the daughter. Me, he says I'm a bastard, a hoodlum like my father. It's hard to take, honestly, but that's the way it is! He's nasty, my uncle-my-mother's-brother, but I really and truly love Malika a lot.

So I pass by my uncle-my-mother's-brother's house, I hide, I want to see Malika. The door is always closed, I go near the windows and see nothing, hear nothing, I'm always ready to run, and when the door opens a little, I do. Only once did I hear her laugh, ah, that made me happy, and another time I saw her, one night when there was light, she came out tottering and muttering things, and I really couldn't sleep, she can talk now, my tiny little sister, she knows how to talk and I told Momo and all my friends: 'She's talking, my little sister, and I'll see her again soon, I'll even kiss her, oh yeah, nobody will keep me from kissing her,' I really couldn't sleep that night.

I wake up very early every Friday morning and slip behind Father Moud who's off to greet his dead. He doesn't see me, he walks straight ahead mumbling things and I stop at the cemetery gate, I don't know where Mama is, I can't ask anyone, but I know she's there and so I do what Father Moud does, I talk very quietly, I know she's listening, I tell her I love her and that I love Malika, that I have no more stomachaches, that the house is still locked, that it's empty, that my uncle, her brother, doesn't like me and our cousins don't like me but it's alright, I'm with Father Moud, our neighbor who's a good man and Momo, his big son, is my friend, make no mistake about it, he's no scoundrel, he's my friend, that's all. And then I tell her that one day when I'm strong, I will work and bring beautiful stones for her tomb, 'cause I'm going to find it, that's for sure. I don't talk to her about Papa, or our games, or about the school I've quit, no, she wouldn't be happy about that and I'd much rather see her smile, Mama, her beautiful white smile, her dimples getting deeper, her eyes lighting up, no, I only tell her that I'm fine and that I watch Malika from the distance and won't leave her and that when I'm grown I'll take her with me, and then I know she's happy wherever she is up there, and I leave before Father Moud sees me and lectures me, and I feel good, and then I can run to see my buddies.

THE FATHER

You who are my Life,

No, I knew nothing when I chided you, when I shouted at you, when I begged the darkness to move away from you, when I hugged you too hard to tear you away from everything, I knew nothing. I should have just kissed your hands, your whole body, and the soles of your feet and thanked God for having met you, I should have devoted my life to following your shadow everywhere and listening to your voice.

It's dark today, the sun's rays are struggling to slide across our walls, the gusts of wind are singing outside, the electricity has gone out, it's with trembling hand and rolling eyes that I write you, but nothing can stop me from reaching out to caress your unattainable presence. We dig in inside our cells like cold and hungry beasts. We hear no voices, only snoring. My friend Diallo isn't singing, my 'protector' Ali has forgotten about me a little, he's hiding under a filthy, patched-up blanket. We almost miss the long days of the heatwave when we'd turn in circles driven mad by heat and humidity. Now it's the cold and the wind that make us miserable. Do you remember our windy days? You'd be swearing, you'd refuse to go out, you'd curse the nasty climate. I was always taught to respect the weather, the weather is God, I said, that's what I was always taught.

Now I no longer pay any attention to the sky. Since you've left there is no sky anymore. It has vanished and the stars have scattered. It was there throughout my childhood, it would watch me through the cracks in our tents, under the shade of our palm trees, it would bellow with blazing heat during the day and turn into a canvas of clarity and life at night. I've never known how to live without it. You know how I'd always leave a window half-open at home, day and night, I need to feel the sky in order to feel me.

Feel me? You'd rant and rail if you saw me today, you'd rip my clothes off and drag me into the shower, the way you used to when I came back from the mine.

They came here, my friends from the mine, there's Dramé, whom you knew, the one whose little finger was cut off, there's Sidna, who's very funny but he wasn't laughing yesterday, and then my friend Omar, the trade unionist, they brought me clothes and some money, they expressed their empathy, their concern, their solidarity, and more. Dramé had tears in his eyes, I told them that I was in a different place, that none of that could be of use to me anymore, that others might need these, they didn't react at all, they simply left without taking their gifts. I handed everything out to the other prisoners. I don't need anything, all I need is you...

It's true, I need you. I felt it for the first time when the tear gas bombs were silenced and I had to leave, something in my heart and head was calling for you, bewildered, I couldn't stay in place, I saw you every moment. The next day I came back, do you remember? To thank your mother, I claimed. You opened the door and you laughed when you saw me: 'Oh, it's you? No police on your trail?' I said no and tried to laugh as well. Your mother wasn't home, I wanted to wait for her, you made tea. And because I had nothing to say, didn't have the courage to talk about you, I wanted to explain my political commitment, I spoke to you about colonialism, neo-colonialism, imperialism. 'What's all that,' you said, still laughing, 'are those djinns, monsters?' I cited names, Ho Chi Minh, Guevara, Mandela. 'All old men, right?' You were making fun of me.

And then I brought up the issues of poverty, the misery of the people and, worried, you asked me: 'Are you from a poor family?' I said no, first backpedaling, the first challenge to my identity. I didn't want to be what you very clearly didn't want me to be. 'As for me,' you went on, 'I know poverty and I abhor it. It's never pretty when you're hungry, when your mother sings little songs into your ears so you won't hear your growling stomach complain anymore; when she lights a fire under a pot filled with water so you'll be quiet and fall asleep as you're waiting; when the other girls all wear brightly colored dresses and you go to school in mended clothes; when you borrow earrings from your friends and are obliged to give them back; when you see your once beautiful mother wilt under her never-ending, badly paid work as a seamstress. Yes, I abhor poverty and I want to get away from it once and for all. Since my brother has become an adult and has been working, things are better, he provides the basics, we're not hungry anymore, I dress like other people, but I dream of going out into the world, wearing beautiful clothes, driving a car, really traveling, not just through books; no, I wouldn't marry a poor man for anything in the world.' I was completely stunned by your words and by the allure that was shimmering in your eyes, my darling, I saw you walk away from me, run through green pastures that my harsh drought couldn't compete with. And I wanted to move close to you and hold on to you, no matter what.

Ah yes, that was the day when my fabrications started, I sketched a story for you that wasn't mine, I wanted to come across as a suitable lover. I concealed my life from you, I rejected the generous ideas I thought I believed in and that were now embarrassing me, I claimed I could offer you anything. Now that the noise around you has been silenced, now that you have taken your dreams away with you, maybe you'll listen, understand, forgive.

My brother wanted me to go to the city to study, to 'be someone'. One fine morning, we were on the road, well, on the dunes. I remember it well, it was still dark when we left, it was cold, too, that burning cold that loves to clasp you very strongly early in the morning, take advantage of dawn's sweetness before the sun returns and spreads its hot breath over our lands all day long. We walked for a long time, I was sniffling a little because I didn't want to leave our camp, or my friends, or our games, and because they had forewarned me: 'Over there they know nothing about anything, not about eating, drinking, playing, praying, singing, over there they don't know how to love, they don't know how to laugh wholeheartedly, they suffocate beneath stone and cement ceilings, their language is as cold as the food of the djinns, and their looks are made of stone like the hearts of the legendary ogres, and there's no morality there either, there are thieves and murderers everywhere.' I didn't want to die, I was especially afraid of becoming a *bezgui*, a city child who doesn't know how to speak.

We went to stay with some cousins and after a few days my brother left me behind with these people whom I didn't know. It's true that I had nothing to complain about. Amed and his wife didn't have any children and quickly adopted me, were concerned about feeding me well, about my clothes, and my studies, above all. I, too, became attached to them. They were kind and considerate, they didn't treat me like their son but rather like a younger brother you know how to listen to and understand. And it was beautiful to behold, this childless couple that loved each other so tenderly, that loved to watch each other live, feeling the other at their side in a country where procreation is considered to be the ultimate goal of marriage. They had defied everyone, their own families, who were convinced they should separate to perhaps have children with someone else. But one day I heard Amed say: 'I prefer a single moment with Amina over any children that another woman might give me.'

Where school was concerned, I quickly caught up since I had learned the practice of reciting from the Koranic school, plus, I wanted to please this couple whom I had come to love. My brother, on the other hand, had emigrated, gone to trade in Central Africa, mostly to smuggle. One of our old traditions. He'd outlined a plan for himself and for me. I was to become an educated man familiar with modern-day things, speaking foreign languages, becoming a lawyer later on, or an administrator. He expected me to be the brains of the camp, who'd help with his advice, who'd put pressure on the administrations, who might bring back projects, aid, or subsidies, who'd defend the tribe's interests in word and in action. Having become rich, he would ensure the camp's survival, support it with his money, dig wells if necessary. He believed that the era of nomadism was finished, that the camp had to choose a place where it could settle without disbanding, that we should stay together. He didn't want to see the camp disappear or break apart, he refused to accept the signs of the times: dispersion or destitution. Settle down somewhere, close to the main roads but far from the cities, stay together no matter what. My brother is a man of loyalty and, rest assured, a man of his convictions, too.

■ ■ ■

Shut up! Shut the hell up! They refuse to quiet down, these uncouth prisoners, they're deaf, they don't hear your voice humming a song by Dimi, that delicious voice of Dimi mingling with yours, as when you'd sing along with the radio in the kitchen, I'd see you from the back, your hair kissing your neck, your body gently swaying to the rhythm, peeling potatoes, finishing a chore as old as the world with lightness and grace.

You didn't like chores, my darling, no, that's not a reproach, I promise, it's simply true; you never liked working, you loathed physical exertion, you loathed bad smells, and then—above all—you loathed your childhood that had consisted of perpetual toil. You felt that a beautiful woman should simply remain beautiful, not be allowed to fade, that physical work was the curse of men and that they alone should carry its load. Yet, you adored our children, you loved seeing them clean, healthy, you...

I am not forgetting our children, no, I love them too much to forget them, but I want them to stop thinking about us, to retreat from our sorrows, to make a way through life that's not covered with the thorns of our suffering. They shouldn't wear the palm wreaths of pain around their heads that we wrapped around ours, may they forget us so they can live, can grow up, and may they erase the cruel stigmata of our tragic destiny from their hearts.

Our son is with my friend Moud again, our neighbor. He's a man of extraordinary goodness. True, you didn't like him very much, you said he was ignorant, too coarse, with 'the manners and mind of a dock-worker', you never probed the core of the man, a paragon of good will. I met him at the time that I wanted to change the world, we became really close, he hadn't studied, he had a vision of humanity that was perhaps naïve but very generous. He is a proud man who does not put up with injustice. Only, life has shackled him, penury and new responsibilities have crushed him, he was no longer free to go where he wanted and found himself to be a prisoner of his situation. He was circling inside a cage and couldn't bury his pride, that's where the rage comes from that's always inside him but it hides a heart of gold. He is very poor and has many children, but he will love our son and he'll protect him.

You know, when I saw my child in the visiting room, I almost fell apart, I felt the boundless burden of my failure. There he was, looking at me as if with a single tap of a magic wand I was going to make everything whole again, you, the years, the happiness. His eyes and tears clung to me and I, I couldn't do anything anymore, the tragic event had passed, there wasn't anything else I could do anymore. So I held him in my arms very tightly and asked him not to come back. I have already left, my name shouldn't appear on the registers of time, for the sake of him my son and for the others. I should exist for no one but you.

My life no longer matters to me. I'm finished, and the living do not ask the opinion of those who are dead. Even our children no longer belong to us. I have lost everything and I accept that, I have no other future but you, who has become the past for all others.

Last night, I saw you in my dream, you were opening your arms and a cloud separated us. I tried to cross the mists to come to you, I held out my hand to grasp you, kiss the edge of your veil, but the immaculate whiteness seemed impenetrable. I threw myself with all my might on the barrier of fog that separated us, but I ran into a bronze wall, I called out your name above the clouds, I said that I loved you, that I wanted to join you, you smiled and looked away, I called again with all the power I had so you would hear me, but your eyes were gazing at a distant star that I could not perceive; and then, very slowly, you slipped away, taking with you an infinite trail of stars.

I'm telling you about me as if you didn't know everything, as if my story hadn't flayed you alive, as if you weren't counting your wounds like so many proofs of my lies, my arrogance, my madness in wanting you by my side, at any price. But listen to me once again...

I wasn't a bad student, I had many friends, I'd become quite 'urbanized', I'd learned to dress like the rest, speak like the rest, I'd hum tunes that were popular, I had wide-ranging ideas and tight-fitting clothes, I went to the movies and sometimes to a concert, I frequented libraries, lived with a loving family, but I was bored. That life seemed bland to me, I didn't have any dreams, any horizon to head for, they'd destined me for knowledge, for becoming an executive, a high-ranking official or something like that, but I didn't want to embrace those ambitions, I found them drab, like the streets I crossed every day to go to school, like the courses they flung at me, like the people's speeches and their vile concerns. I found the life there in our desert more fascinating, the people more real, the relationships warmer. The smiles of young girls were more eloquent, they'd make our hearts throb, and then, too, we were always waiting – waiting for rain, grass, the animals to return, a love in the process of blossoming, a well to be dug, new camps to be settled a few dozen kilometers away, a journey, maybe some beautiful eyes. We, we know how to wait, and every moment of the day is the promise of a gift.

It was out of boredom that I embraced the cause of some of my friends who wanted to change everything. They insulted the government, they accused the West and the corrupt African regimes of all evil, they promised to wash the wounds of the people in a revolution that would sweep away all selfishness and cause happiness to flourish.

I liked the camaraderie that I encountered with them, the complicity that was born from clandestine action and also the brazen ideology that broke with all our traditions and promised a new dawn that I knew to be impossible. I participated in demonstrations, distributed pamphlets, read big books that I found difficult to understand but which broke with all our beliefs, I was brimming with a new faith that was going to turn the world upside down. There were strikes, demonstrations, sit-ins, police beatings, days in prison, and the feeling of being a hero. But all this was held together by a thread that promptly broke when I met you.

■ ■ ■

Ali woke up. He stands up and stretches like a king. We make the coffee that he and I will drink alone. The others will wait. Ali is a leader. He looks around and everyone is silent. At breakfast time he demands silence. His gaze is fierce and only softens a little with me. At such moments I am the sole person who can break the silence. He has selected me to be his friend, his protégé. His marabou as well. 'He's an intellectual and he knows the Koran', those words sound like a blessing coming from his mouth. In his eyes I'm almost a saint, and a hero, too.

Ali is a regular in the prison system, he's been convicted for assault, burglary, rape, drug trafficking, all of it. He's a violent man, possessed by a rage that can't be stifled. All the prisoners are afraid of him. Yes, my darling, the values here are not the ones we know, here it's strength, cruelty, physical daring that are respected. Ali always has a sharpened blade on him that can be plunged into someone's body in a flash. Nobody would accuse him, not even the one whom he attacked: he has inscribed people's foreheads with fear. Gang leader outside the prison, inside he surrounds himself with an organized pack. They have everything, cigarettes, food, cell phones, money, and the support of the guards. But, oddly, this hot-headed and ignorant gang leader claims to have faith, says his five daily prayers, and on Fridays he demands that every prisoner go to the common prayer. He also likes to listen to poetry, he loves it when I sometimes recite the verses by Ould Addebbe, the Tagant poet. Surely you remember how in the evening we both loved to listen to the now deceased griot Cheikh Ould Abba as he sang his poems of oases and love in his pure and wistful voice.

> *Willingly or not, the eyes' tears*
> *Will flow for the beloved woman*
> *And for the tribe, which vanished yesterday,*
> *They will flow*
> *Willingly or not*

So, I've made a friend here, in spite of myself, one of those friendships that is forced upon you. It's true, my darling, we don't always choose our friends. After meeting you I split with my fellow fighters. They had a dim view of this 'petit-bourgeois' love that was getting in the way of my revolutionary action and I, I was growing tired of their convictions, I no longer came to meetings, no longer participated in demonstrations, our ties slackened, and then completely stopped. In and of itself friendship is not enough in very committed environments.

I was possessed by you and could no longer see any other possible passion. I didn't go to the university anymore, I didn't go home to my guardians until very late, I devoted most of my time to you. I struggled to appear like a 'good' person in your eyes. At first, I borrowed money from my friends, my guardians, the shopkeepers I knew, then I wrote to my brother who sent me a money order to settle my debts, I sold my belongings. I wanted to see you happy, fill the awful lack of beautiful things that had hollowed you out inside. You couldn't conceive of love without proof, to really love a woman means to spoil her, fulfill her desires, you said. I made every effort to meet your expectations and I was well compensated in return: seeing you jump for joy, your arms around me, your laughter swirling inside me, your gaze fixed on mine, all this exuberance was worth any of the world's treasures. Your mother accepted me, she wasn't very old, maybe around fifty, but life had worn her down, already unsteady and half blind. She knew my tribe very well and sometimes told me legends about my people that I didn't know or thought I'd forgotten. I would stay with you all day long. You weren't going to class anymore, but you were preparing for your final exams from high school, with which I'd help you a little, although I could tell that your appetite for academics was nonexistent.

Do you remember $E = mc^2$, my love? We really liked that old formula and satirized it often. 'Existentialism is a humanism, my love', 'I think of you, so I exist in you, my life', 'the Bastille fell one July 14ᵗʰ, my heart', we created a thousand formulas that made us laugh and were a prelude to lengthy kisses. At night I had to leave again because your brother was coming home from work. I ran into him once or twice and he gave me a suspicious, arrogant look. He's a man rife with prejudices, he says he's attached to the old values, religious sanctions, but the only thing that moves him is his own vanity and his desire to appear 'proper' in the eyes of others. He never liked me, your brother. He never even liked you either, or your mother; he definitely worked hard to keep you two alive but it was only to give himself the appearance of being a 'good son' down here and make sure the gates of paradise would be opened for him. That's your brother: he's afraid of how others see him down here and of how God sees him up there, and he loves nothing but himself. That's why he was always opposed to our happiness.

You know, forbidden love is almost a common thing, novels are full of it, newspapers, too, they'll give you thousands of examples of it in every neighborhood. Our stories and our poetry are packed with impossible passions! Do you remember Abd Messouma? I loved telling you his story. He was a slave who had fallen madly in love with his mistress. He was in terrible agony.

> *How many more nights will all the others sleep*
> *While I, insomniac, am aching for you*

There where you are now, do you sometimes repeat these lines you loved so much? Our poet managed to escape and change his identity. He went as far as Oualata, the city of wisdom, to acquire knowledge and go back to his masters wearing the white turban and the aura of an *ulema*, he was unrecognizable, except to his beloved. He married his former owner and they lived happily after. You liked love stories that end well. I can tell you thousands of them, drawn from all the books and languages in existence, but ours is special because it's ours and because each love affair is unique.

We were wild, of course, we'd laugh at the taboos, we thought we were above petty contingencies, and we loved loving each other everywhere, every second, every time we were out of the sight of others. But it didn't take you long to become rattled, start to panic, and weep all the time because you thought you were pregnant; I didn't give it much thought, I believed we were protected, that our good Lord loved us, that we were shielded from misfortune because we were innocent. Weren't we? But then it became a reality when a loathsome doctor told you, smiling widely: 'Congratulations Madame, it's a boy.' You swore you would die. 'In any case, my brother will kill me', you screamed, I swore I'd live and die with you. And, in the end, we saw that to get married was the only way out. Ultimately, you held that hasty wedding against me: 'I hadn't lived enough yet, I was too young.' But I, too, was very young. Not even twenty-five! But did we have any choice? I spoke to your mother, who already knew. She opened her heart to your brother, who refused at first but then had to give in. My family went into a tailspin. I wasn't asking their permission, I had no need of that. What I demanded was that I receive my whole share of the inheritance. My brother yelled at me on the phone, I informed my uncle who took offense at my impatience. They felt I was too young to manage a herd, three hundred camels to look after, feed, deal with, care for, sell but only when the time is ripe and, more than all of that, they were a luxury. 'They belong to you, that's true, but actually they belong to the entire camp, several families live on it. If everyone were to withdraw their animals it would be the end, and besides, what about your studies...'

I didn't want to hear any of it, I threatened to sue them. I kept repeating that the law was on my side. They grew angry, cried infamy, ingratitude, betrayal, the killing of my father, but they had to give in. I then inquired about the price of livestock, went to a trader— the father of one of my friends—who offered me a tidy sum. I never dreamed of having that much money, millions, my darling. You see, nomads aren't all that poor, it's just that in their eyes wealth doesn't lie in millions, it's the livestock you caress in the morning and see return at night.

Ah yes, speaking of millions... a truly hilarious story that my friends at the mine told me. Right after my arrest, the company executives published a photograph of me wearing a helmet, smiling, with arms raised as if reacting to an ovation, and the caption below it said: 'We are happy because we create.' The photo appeared on every site in the country and beyond. These advertising people had picked a photo from among hundreds and had no idea who I was, just some worker among thousands of others. They'd been tricked by my good looks, by the smile that happened to be a broad one just then (perhaps I was happy at that instant because I was thinking of you). Bosses never read local papers, they don't speak its language. So they didn't know about me. Of course, they were compelled to withdraw the photo and even to apologize to the public. You don't flaunt a criminal. My friends wanted me to lodge a complaint about the picture and about the apologies: they had no right to reproduce my photograph without my permission, nor did they have the right to apologize as if I'd already been sentenced, while I hadn't been judged yet and was therefore presumed innocent. They explained to me that I could make millions. But no, that's not in my nature, I don't feel like fighting a pointless battle that I would surely lose, and I don't feel like taking advantage of the idiocy of others, even of the powerful, I live too much inside myself to make any demands, to keep protesting. No! And besides, what would I do with those millions? Even when I was free, I was never hungry for money, unless it was a matter of satisfying you.

Still, selling my livestock was very valuable to us, those bundles of bills, the fruit of millions of hours of nomadism, millions of hours of care, millions of hours of anxiety and fear, millions of years of know-how. 'It's an entire past history that I've sold,' I told myself in my moments of despondency, but I wouldn't think of it that often, especially not when you were there beside me.

How beautiful you were the evening of our wedding! Your hairstyle, high and sprinkled with pearls, coming down to your chest, your henna-dyed hands and feet, your weightless veil of a rich Oriental fabric, and that faraway glance that befits young brides and made you look like a captivating, unapproachable queen. I strutted around by your side, in a totally white boubou, a black turban around my head, a triumphant smile; with my arm around you in front of everyone, as if to let them know that: 'from now on, she belongs to me, she is mine.' We had invited the most popular griots, even the diva Dimi was there, who enthralled the audience and who actually thought you were 'too beautiful for me'—I overheard it. You wanted a splendid wedding, my darling, and you got one.

When I think about that evening, I sometimes tell myself that we took too large a portion of happiness then, in just a single night. Yes, my darling, perhaps happiness comes in segments, wisely spread throughout a life by the hand of destiny, so one ought not to overindulge in it, one ought to leave some portions for the future. Maybe that's what it is: we were just so happy that night, and during the following days and months, we rushed on to that lush roast lamb of love, we swallowed huge mouthfuls of bliss, and perhaps that's when we consumed our whole ration of happiness. 'Nonsense!' you'd say again. And yet...

THE SON

I used to think that our house was our home, it's where we were born, me and Malika, and then there was Mama, Papa, me and Malika, that's it. It was ours. But no, after 'it' happened, a long time after, people came and cleaned, removed the shit, swept in front of the door, me, I was watching and said to myself: 'This isn't normal, that's our house!' It hurt, but Momo explained: 'It's been rented, it's for some guy who doesn't even live in PK7, it's not for you.' I didn't get it: it was our house and then 'it' happened.

I go to the big prison every week, I don't get too close, no, I watch from far away, that's all, I sit under a tree and I watch, often there's nobody but me and the trees and the guards in front of the prison, but Papa is there in the back, I know, it's where he lives and he doesn't budge, he told me not to come, but I come anyway, from a distance like this, without him seeing me, same as for Mama. Except that Mama is dead and Papa is over there.

It's big, Papa's prison, very big, and the walls are very high, the gate is enormous and when it opens the noise hurts your ears, I notice another door and I see people, but it goes too fast, I can't make anything out. Except one day I saw someone who looked like Papa, he was wearing something casual, his feet were shackled and he was hopping, he looked like Papa I tell you, except it only lasted a minute, and slam, the gate closed and then it was over. If it's Papa, I told myself, he'll tell the guard: 'My son is here', and the guards will call and let me in; I waited for a long time but the guards didn't call me, so I told myself that it couldn't have been Papa.

As for me, deep inside I still believe that Papa did nothing wrong, but I don't say that to anyone, not even to Momo because the one time I did he answered: 'Be quiet, you're talking nonsense!', I kept quiet but I still believe it anyway!

Why doesn't Papa want to see me?

'It's because he feels remorseful when he sees you', Momo claims. It's not true, I know it.

Father Moud took me to see Papa only once, we waited in front of the gate for a long time, then we went inside, waited some more, and Papa came, he'd changed, he was skinny, he wore dirty clothes, his eyes were big and red and right away he hugged me very tight, too tight, it hurt, I almost cried, then he told Father Moud: 'Don't bring him anymore, he's not to come back here again, send him back to his uncle, my brother, down where the campsites are, he must not come here again!' then he pushed me away, quickly turned around, the door slammed and I shouted 'Papa!' and Father Moud dragged me outside, that's how it was, yes, that's exactly how it was, that time I cried but Papa didn't come back and that really hurt, hurt a lot, sobs were sticking in my throat, there were tears everywhere, on my neck and my shirt and I even felt something in my pants, I swear, I stayed home a long time, I didn't move, then I thought: 'I'll go see Papa every week, I'll sit under the trees, and I'll wait for him at a distance, maybe he'll come out one day, he has to, and he'll come over and kiss me like before, he will, and maybe we'll even go back home again.'

We always go to the sea on Saturdays, there's a lot of people, especially at the fish market, people and fish everywhere, they're in a hurry, we go in, some fish are as big as me and others are tiny, some have their mouths open and look at you, it's scary, some look like they're sleeping, some are still moving a little, and there are always very rich grand ladies who come to buy and we ask: 'May I help you?' and we lug their huge bags to the car and the ladies always give us coins, sometimes even a bill, and sometimes they tell us to scrape off the fish scales and we have knives and we scrape and scrape, and the ladies pay us some more. They're always very beautiful, those grand ladies who come to the beach on Saturdays.

Me, when I go home from the beach, I always bring back a bit of fish for Sara, it makes Momo laugh, but Sara is happy, she even kisses me on my cheeks and when I smell the whiff of her perfume close up something happens inside me, and sometimes I become very sad but then later on I'm happy. Momo doesn't like Sara, because she doesn't talk to him, he says things to her but she doesn't say a word back, and she doesn't even say anything to the others, she looks straight ahead, except with me, and sometimes the kids say: 'Look, there's Sara, she's carrying something in her basket, you should ask', and me, I don't answer, I won't even do it, not even for Momo!

One time little Selma became sick, she cried, which wasn't normal, she never cries. Mother Maria was tired, she was fast asleep, Father Moud wasn't even there, so I touched Selma's head, it was hot, very hot, I knew it: it was a fever, before, little Malika always had fevers; so I woke up Mother Maria, then Momo, and we left for the hospital, it was night, it was far, there wasn't any bus, just taxis, which cost too much, so we walked, there was no one on the street except us, but Momo had a knife and me, I had my pocketknife, Momo was carrying Selma, Mother Maria had her baby in her arms, and I was walking beside her. At the hospital a guy told us to pay, Mother Maria answered: 'No, we can't pay, we have nothing!', so he looked at us and let us in. They laid Selma on a very white bed, stuck a needle in her arm, and a long tape, and even something to help her breathe, then she fell asleep, we were watching her, she was so cute. Mother Maria asked Momo and me to go back home because the other kids were all alone. In the morning Momo bought bread for the children but at noon there was nothing left to eat anymore, Tenn and Toto were crying, so then I saw Sara go by and I talked to her. She brought us a large bowl with a lot of rice and fish, and we ate everything, and when she came back to pick up the empty bowl, Sara even touched my cheek, oh, I was so happy, Momo said: 'You're like her little brother', but I didn't answer, I was just happy, that's all.

When Father Moud came back that night he had some money and we had another meal. Momo went off to the hospital to bring some portions to his mother and little sister. We were able to see Selma two days later, she opened her eyes and me and Momo pinched her cheek, a little too hard just to see, she didn't cry, she just muttered very softly, 'Ichi' and 'Ichou', that was good, she was better.

My baby sister Malika was sick all the time, she had all kinds of trouble, especially with her stomach, but she had fever also and sometimes she'd throw up, then old Vara would come, who scared me with her big bun of hair, her very wrinkled skin, and that face that didn't smile. She'd often pick Malika up by her little feet, hold her upside down, and plunk her into a bowl of water. Malika would scream and I'd feel like screaming, too, and chase her away, but it was all for Malika's good, I think I understood there was something in her body that had to come back out. Then Papa would give the old woman a coin. Sometimes Malika got better very quickly, sometimes not, so then Papa would take her to the hospital and buy medications, which were very expensive, he'd always say: 'Those pharmacists are crooks, they eat people alive.' I told that to Momo once: 'Pharmacists eat people', and he laughed, treated me like an idiot, I said nothing. There are things he just doesn't know, Momo.

But when she wasn't sick, Malika, she was good for me, made my heart happy, and I'd be laughing all the time, she'd squirm a lot and laugh in her little crib, she'd touch my nose and, when she started to crawl on all fours, she was on the move all the time, I'd always be behind her to catch her. She was fast and the two of us would laugh and one time she even went outside, we didn't see her, the door was open, she'd gone out and Mama yelled, looked for her everywhere and I was scared, really scared, but someone found her outside scurrying ahead on all fours, and brought her back, and Mama hugged her tight and cried, but Malika was happy and laughing. That was a little before 'it'.

When Papa wasn't there, Mama was on the telephone, that's all, and a gentleman would come to pick us up and take us to the clinic and he'd pay for everything. Mama had a lot of friends and they were all very nice to us, I wanted to tell Papa to act like Mama, but I couldn't. Every day she'd repeat the same thing: 'If you say one word about what I do to Papa, I'm leaving, and I'm leaving you here.' I didn't want to lose Mama.

I really liked Mama's friends, they were all nice, except one whose name was Cheib, he was always there when Papa was at work, he had ways about him, he always made a strange gesture with his hands and he talked a lot and kissed Malika too much, he'd carry her around, I'd always tell him: 'Leave my sister alone' and he'd answer that I was as nasty as my father.

Another one, Mady, he was the fattest, he was very nice. He always brought presents for me and Malika, he'd carry Malika on his shoulders and dance, she'd laugh and I would too, and then he'd sing in a language we didn't know, but it was wonderful and we all danced together. Often Mama would shout at him: 'Mady, you're like a child!' Mama's voice... I still have it in my ears, Mama's voice, it's like when a fine drizzle caresses your head, Mama's voice, or like when you're cold and wearing a nice warm burnous or like... I don't know, I'm just saying things, but it made me feel good, Mama's voice.

My Mama was beautiful, everyone said so, even people in the street used to tell her: 'You're beautiful!', she didn't answer, just smiled a little; her clothes were always clean and fine and they smelled good, I loved to put my head in them, those multicolored veils and dresses that nobody in the neighborhood wore. The people of PK7 would sometimes talk very softly, whispering things, but they were just jealous she said, it's true, and even Sara told me once: 'She was beautiful, your mother.'

Sara is also very beautiful, you know, I love watching her, just to watch, and when she walks, you'd say it isn't our area, she sees none of the filth, none of the rot, none of the dark earth, you'd say she walks on carpets like the women in soap operas do, she holds her head high, her basket on her arm, and she's swaying when she walks. Sara, when I see her that way something inside me always moves, and I'm happy when she calls me, I run, of course I run, and all the kids are jealous, I know, but it's always me she calls and Momo keeps telling me: 'She takes you for a kid'. I know it: Momo is jealous, too, but—whatever!

Sara often declares: 'You're like my brother, be careful, don't become a scoundrel or a thief like those horrible kids in PK7, you should go to school, pray at the mosque and all that, and think of your future so you don't end up as a carrier or a dock-worker or an orderly or a guard or as nothing at all, like the men in PK7, you should study for your future, the future, the future, she loves repeating that, Sara does, the future, me I don't answer, I just nod to keep Sara happy, but that doesn't mean I don't think about it.

■ ■ ■

My Papa took me to the fair sometimes, to see the lion. There were other animals, too, but the lion is the strongest Papa told me, he roamed around his cage like a a big chief and opened his mouth wider than anything, wider than I or even Momo, and he'd roar, very loud, it used to scare me. There was a crocodile, too, sleeping in the water and birds who hopped around in their prison. Papa would get angry: 'It's disgraceful, the lion doesn't get enough to eat, he'll die, these folks they're thieves.' Papa treats everyone like a thief, even those who sell things for a pittance, he says they should just give it to the poor. The government people are thieves as well. Once I saw a big guy on television, he didn't smile, he was clenching his teeth, he looked as if he were peeing: 'Who's that?' 'It's someone from the government.' When I asked: 'Why isn't he in prison, Papa, he's a thief, isn't he?' Papa laughed, he kissed me, he always kisses me, Papa does, when I don't understand something.

When Papa comes home, it's the end of television me and Mama used to say. Papa would only watch the news and politics, and Mama would protest, but he wouldn't listen, he'd leave the soap opera on for a bit but just as it would get interesting, he'd change the channel, then Mama would yell at him: 'No, you've already seen the news, and politics, it's always the same stuff.'

When there's something political, us kids of PK7 we're happy, people gather, lots of people, and we run to the center, the people treat us like ruffians but we have a good time, there's music and dancing, there's money, too, they give us some change to keep us quiet, so we won't steal the mikes and wires, and even to shut us up or have us shout: 'Down with the president, down with the president', 'Long live the president, long live the president'. We paste photographs on the walls and rip them off again, all of it for money, and there's always drinks to be had, Coke, Sprite, Evian, anything we want and cake, too. Father Moud doesn't like all this, he's like Papa, he treats them like thieves. One day Momo and I took Selma by the hand and went out onto the street, a photographer saw us and gave us a large photo and a flag, he gave us coins and then took a picture of us, Selma was so cute, she was laughing with her decayed teeth and she was even wearing pants that day, I didn't have a shirt on but I had my shoes, and Momo was well dressed, he was playing 'Ronaldo', and we thought it was fine. But a few days later Father Moud came home enraged, he had the newspaper with our photo and was angry, which we didn't understand, it was a good picture, our photo, but father Moud was really mad, he took us to the police to complain, he took us very far away to some offices to shout, we were tired but didn't say so, we were afraid. 'They even steal the images of our children', father Moud said. When Momo asked: 'Who does, who steals?' he yelled at him: 'Shut your mouth!'

One day at the cemetery, I saw my uncle-my-mother's-brother, so I hid, he's coming to see Mama I'm sure, I'll follow him, I'm going to find out where Mama is, but I couldn't because he moved along very fast and because I was scared that he'd spot me. As soon as he sees me, he yells, he calls me an 'assassin's son', he won't look at me, I have the feeling he'd like to hit me. I watched him from afar, I was hiding behind a tomb, then a man shouted at me: 'What are you doing here, this is not for children.' My uncle-my-mother's-brother came back, he ran into father Moud without looking at him. Why doesn't he like me?

When I used to go to his house, before, with Mama and Malika, he would never kiss me. I used to play with his son Karim, he's nasty, Karim, he doesn't know anything, he has rabbits and a rooster and when I'd touch them he would cry and Mama would yell at me: 'Leave your cousin alone!'

'He's not my cousin.'

Mouna is the name of the wife of my uncle-my-mother's-brother, she's fat and has a behind like this, but she prepares good meals and you eat well at her house, that's probably why she's so fat, and she talks a lot, she'd tell Mama everything and Mama would laugh. She had a beautiful laugh, Mama did; when I think of that today, it's like music, it goes up a little, then comes down, and her eyes would glisten, like water, it hurts when I think about it.

At night I sometimes scream in my sleep, I didn't believe it at first but Momo insists that it's true—'You scream during the night'—I can't help it, in my head I see Papa and Mama screaming, too, and Mama is almost naked and Papa's running around the house and I say nothing, I just cry. When I wake up I'm scared and father Moud comes to touch my head and he whispers words to me, softly, and I take his hand so I don't have to be afraid anymore and then I fall asleep again.

■ ■ ■

The night when 'it' happened I was asleep, Mama had asked me to go into the other bedroom, I wasn't scared to be alone, I saw Mama's stories come and go on the ceiling, and the ones that Papa and the actors on TV would tell and even those at the Play, because I was already going to the Play. My mother used to say that it was for crooks, but sometimes I'd go there when she went to the market or when she'd go out with her friends. The night that 'it' happened I was asleep, I was in my dream, I saw things, I swear, it's awful, I saw a huge monster, a lizard larger than our house, was watching me, its eyes were very red, I was scared, and then suddenly I woke up and I heard screams, it wasn't a dream, it was Papa's voice. I thought Papa was at work, Mama was yelling also and crying and I was scared, I knocked on the door but it didn't open and Mama was crying very loudly and said: 'I swear to you, I swear to you…' and something else and Papa was shouting and you could hear 'crack, crack', loud noises, and Mama screaming again, and I was going crazy, I was knocking on the door and calling 'Papa! Papa!', he didn't hear it and I was hot, too, sweating all over, and I even wet myself, I swear, I was so scared, I heard Malika crying and I was also yelling 'Malika! Malika!', and it went on for a long time, a very long time, and I couldn't breathe anymore, I was hurting all over. I didn't hear Mama anymore, just Papa who was shouting, still shouting, then people, lots of people, and the door opened, and someone took me in his arms and put his hand over my eyes and everyone was talking, talking, and I was shouting 'Papa! Mama!', but I couldn't see anything because of the hand of the man who carried me away; I felt the cool air outside, the hand loosened up a little, there were many, many people in front of our house, and even a police car, and they were looking at me and someone said: 'Poor kid!' I thought: 'Poor kid, yourself.' But I was really scared, I said to myself: 'They're going to beat me up, they're going to eat me like the big lizard in my dream', and I had a headache, I was just calling 'Papa! Mama!', then someone put a hand over my eyes again, I tried to move my head but he pressed his hand down, then I heard a car leaving and even a woman weeping, I cried, and people even touched my head, I didn't know why. Something very, very serious had happened, I thought without really thinking about it, Mama's left, Papa's left also, and my heart was hurting, my throat too, and I wanted to get away, very far away, forever, then the hand loosened its grip a little and I escaped from everyone, I fled, I was scared, I fled and nobody caught me and I ran all by myself through the empty streets, I ran, I didn't even know where I was, I ran, that's all, and in the end my heart was beating very fast, I was thirsty and I was tired and I thought I was going to die, but I sat down at the foot of a wall and I cried, I didn't know anything but I knew that something had happened, something very horrible, and that Mama and Papa had left forever and little Malika, too, and then I cried some more and fell asleep without knowing why, just like that on the street. Father Moud came I don't know how, he woke me up, carried me in his arms, his voice was choking and he kept saying 'My God, my God!' and I didn't ask anything, I didn't want to know anything and since then I've been living with father Moud, and Momo, who is my friend.

. . .

At night when there's no Play, we'd play *Moriba*, we'd have two teams and we'd hide, then we'd go looking for each other, go behind the doors of the houses, in people's trashcans, we'd lie under parked cars, we'd run around everywhere and people would often yell: 'You're crazy!' and we'd just keep going, keep going. On nights like that, I laughed a lot and I'd come home tired. Only now I don't do that anymore because poor Lemine was running and got hit by a car and I can't describe it for you, no, I can't, there he was just like that on the asphalt, I saw it and threw up and cried, and all the other kids did, too, and his poor mother was weeping and rolling on the ground, and his father, a skinny man who has no tears left in his eyes because he's so old, he kept repeating: '*Ina Llillah, Ina Llillah*', and someone covered Lemine with a white sheet. There were lots and lots of people, the driver had run away, he'd left his car and run away, he was afraid of the crowd, no one saw him, the police came and traced lines with chalk, then an ambulance took poor Lemine away, and we, we were watching from a distance. But when everyone, or almost everyone, was gone, we brought tires, cardboard, gasoline, and we set fire to the car. Momo said that the killer had fled and was on his bed moaning: 'That poor people's poor child, I didn't see him, I was drunk, poor child of PK7, there's nothing but poor people in PK7 in any event, but I gave money, it's over and done with, I can sleep easy now.' We set fire to his car for that reason, for the poor children of PK7. 'And we'll set fire to him if we find him, and to his mother and his father and his mother's mother', Momo added, but someone discouraged us from doing all that. Afterwards no one spoke anymore, there were even kids from PK8 with us, and the flames danced in the sky and the neighborhood was red, it was as if there was electricity everywhere.

■ ■ ■

Sometimes I think: Why am I me? And why is Momo Momo? Each one of us, alone, inside ourselves, I close and then open my eyes: blackness, then sun, blackness, then white, death, then life, why? And why are we poor, and why did Mama leave, and why is Papa in prison, and why am I not grown-up and setting Papa free and why don't I get Malika, and more why, why, why... but then I say to myself: It's no good to think this way for long, it gives you a headache, I should go play or sleep.

Mama loved to sleep all day, she'd close her door and sleep, especially when Papa wasn't there; when Papa was there, she'd wake up and make tea, then she'd get us dressed, go to the kitchen, nurse Malika, but she'd sleep a little when Papa went out. I liked it when Papa was there, I saw Mama all the time, and Papa would tell me lots of things and take me out walking, he'd carry Malika in his arms and I'd walk with them and sometimes I'd run ahead and Malika thought I was leaving forever and she'd cry and I'd come right back dancing like a monkey, Malika would laugh and Papa, too. I liked it a lot when Papa was there and Mama's friends were not, they never came when Papa was home.

Sometimes there are no games at the Play, no soccer, only films from India. I'm not a big fan of those, it makes my heart ache because the actor always has so many problems, they steal his wife or keep her far away from him and he just sings and is miserable. The kids tell me that in the end everything is always fine, the actor kills the crooks and leaves with his beloved, but I always fall asleep before the end, so

Momo tells me what happens and sings the Indian songs, I like that, I don't understand them but it's really nice, I even learned a little bit, just a little, Momo knows them all. Anyhow, in the Indian films you see a lot of flowers, I like seeing the flowers but the others mostly like watching the girls.

I never say anything to the girls of PK7 but, Momo and Mokhis talk to them, they bring them little gifts and the girls laugh, take them, and then they leave. Sometimes the kids write their names on the walls and sometimes other stuff; they follow them but they're afraid because the girls, they always have big brothers and fathers and cousins, tough guys who don't kid around, so Momo and Mokhis follow the girls at a distance and sometimes, but that I haven't seen, it's Momo who told me, they kiss them on the mouth, they say it's great. Anyway, I've never done that; there's just one, her name is Zineb, and she always gives me candy, one time Mokhis spurted: 'She feels sorry for you,' I answered: 'Your mother...!' then ran over to Momo. And Mokhis, there was nothing he could do.

Mbarka is special, she's not really pretty but she's got something, that's what Momo thinks, he talks to her all the time, I dunno, I don't go near her, she scares me a little, she has a husky voice and a big scar on her forehead, she's skinny and always wears a belt around her waist, like this, you see, Mokhis claims it's to show off her breasts. She couldn't care less, she smokes on the street and utters words you shouldn't say out loud, the kids are afraid of her, too, but sometimes she gives them candy, so they keep quiet. Momo is her only friend, they laugh together and sometimes she gives him coins. But Mbarka, she never stays at the PK, she goes off somewhere far away and doesn't come back until evening, sometimes a car drops her off, sometimes it's a taxi, but she always has a package with her, all wrapped up. One time some gentleman came to pick her up, the kids threw stones at him, but Mbarka ran after them and hit them, you don't play around with her, sometimes we call her 'lady with clients', but only among ourselves, you don't play around with her.

But then one day Mbarka wasn't Mbarka anymore, she wore new clothes, bracelets, she built a house for her parents, bought a car, and no longer said hello to anybody. Mbarka wasn't Mbarka anymore, and no one understood, even Momo didn't get it, she no longer said hello even to him, and Meimoune-who-sells-anything says she no longer bought things on credit, she was paying cash and didn't even talk, what happened to her, to Mbarka? We didn't know, some kids said that one of the clients had married her in secret, that does happen, others said she'd stolen many millions from one of her regulars, we knew nothing and then one day she disappeared, we didn't see her anymore, she's rich now abroad somewhere, it seems, with a visa and money and cars and everything, she's doing well, she's lucky, Mbarka, and despite her departure, even if she was nasty sometimes, we're happy for her. Finally someone we know has become a somebody, that's good.

But Django, the owner of the Play, isn't happy, he claims that Mbarka is a bad girl, we don't listen, we know why he says that, because for a long time now Mbarka hasn't come to him behind the Play, in his bedroom, that's over and done with, we talk about it among ourselves, it's over… and we have a good laugh.

One day father Moud ordered Momo: 'Follow me! You're going to work!' and Momo left with him, I waited, I wanted to know and told myself: maybe Momo will become a dock-worker, he's strong, he's going to make money, he'll buy me things, and later on when I'm grown up and will be working also, as a dock-worker, a transporter, or even a cop, a cop is good, I'll set Papa free and I'll build a beautiful tomb for Mama, and I'll put the PK8 and Beyda kids in jail, and I'll marry Sara, being a cop is great. I was laughing and dancing all by myself. But Momo didn't become a dock-worker, no, dock work is for donkeys, they carry stuff on their back, just like donkeys, except for his father, of course. In any case, he became an apprentice for a mechanic, oh yes, he's going to be repairing cars.

The first time he came back completely grimy, his shirt and pants were all black, that's how it is, with men, with work, and he was saying words like 'key', 'rotary cutter', he said 'nut', and he was thrilled. He doesn't get paid yet, Momo, he's just an apprentice for his father's friend, but at noon he eats well, he has soap to wash up with after work, and customers leave him some change, and he also salvages things that other customers throw out, and sells them. Later on he'll be a mechanic and he'll own a car that's all his, that's what he says, Momo.

Papa used to work very far up north, in the mines, I don't know what he did, but he had special work clothes, all buttoned up, and he had enormous glasses, and he was even missing a finger because of his work, but he didn't cry. He's tough, my father, I swear! When he'd come home from work his turban was filled with dust and he had dust in his eyes, it was very far away, his work, the road wasn't paved, it was very far, that's why my father didn't come home every week, only at the end of the month and then just for a few days. He'd say he would take us with him but my mother didn't want that, she said that the schools up there were no good and that it was too hot, that it was bad for children and that she'd get bored, Papa would get angry and sometimes even shout, and I'd be scared, but Mama said no, and when Mama said no it was no.

When Papa came home it was always with money, fruit, meat, a lot of it, I was allowed to invite my friends, Mama didn't like them very much because they were dirty but Papa called all of them 'my children!' and he'd even give them all some coins, he was kind to everyone, Papa was.

My Mama, she didn't like to work, she said she was tired, so sometimes we had a maid, a young maid who'd prepare food and sweep and carry Malika. But Mama always fired them very quickly, except for one whose name was Astou, she was nice, she'd play with me when she had time and she was very scared of Mama, but one day she burned her hand, she cried, Mama took her to the clinic, then to her parents' house, but she didn't come back. Astou used to tell me that her parents were fishermen, that they lived very far away by the little sea and that they knew the fish, that the fish knew them and that they'd toss things in the little sea, and that nobody besides them could fish anymore, was that true? I don't know, and then she'd sometimes show me her thing and ask me if I wanted to be her husband, I said yes, just like that, and she'd laugh very loudly and say: 'You're too young', she was weird, Astou, but she was really very nice.

Some guy with a long beard and sleepy eyes comes to the house, with a book, and he talks softly with father Moud and father Moud listens and even mother Maria sometimes interrupts her cooking and comes to listen, he says things about religion, father Moud and mother Maria nod their head and say: 'That's true', sometimes he even brings them a tape recorder with a cassette, they listen and have tears in their eyes, and that man speaks as if he were singing, and he gently turns his head, smiles and opens his eyes, it makes me laugh that act of his, and besides he's really not good-looking, and when mother Maria hands him some change he never takes it, for him the only reward is in paradise. Father Moud goes to the mosque now and re-cites the Koran very softly, so I told Momo: 'Your father is a good Muslim, he'll go to paradise.' Momo replied: 'You're an idiot, paradise is not for the people of PK7, if God loved us all he'd have to do is send us to Tevragh Zeina, the rich neighborhood, that would be cool, here he puts us in shit because he doesn't like us, we're morons here, and thieves and liars, and there are plenty of whores here.' Me, I answered: 'That's not true!' So he got angry and yelled at me: 'You, you're a fool, or what, you think paradise is for your father or my father or even for my mother who works so hard and does nothing wrong, you think it's for Django who sells joints at the Play and hides girls in his room, back there, you think it's for Meimoune-who-sells-anything and buys stolen objects, or for one-eyed Dahi who reads his book and from be-neath the book looks at the behinds of little girls, you believe it's for us, the PK kids, bastards, thieves, or for our parents, ignorant people who can't even read, and bums who work hard for nothing, or who do nothing for nothing, you think that the good Lord's going to let these shits here defile his beautiful paradise, no, it makes no sense.' I didn't say anything because I know that when Momo is like that you have to let him be, not answer him, he acts like a jerk that's all, let him be, it will pass.

Demba-the-madman, he's no fool. We know that because he's our friend, he tells us stories, oh yes, Demba-the-madman isn't even mad. What he does during the day he does only to earn a little money. It's because of his mother who's blind and has nothing, and because of his brothers, all of them scoundrels who left. He goes on some big avenue into the city with a large stick and a stone and holds out his hand like this in front of cars, saying nothing. People see the stick, they see the giant stone, and they give, it's just safer. Because Demba sometimes touches the windshield with his stick, and even sings and says: 'I love you!' to the windshield, and also: 'You shine like the eyes of my beloved, you really appeal to me!' and then when the driver doesn't give him anything Demba claims he sees the face of the girl who betrayed him in the windshield. 'I'll have to crack that image, I have to', and he raises his stick or his stone and the driver gets scared and gives him something.

At night, Demba sits in front of the shop of Meimoune-who-sells-anything. 'Children, I'm going to tell you a story.' We often don't even listen anymore because Demba's stories are always the same, two or three short tales that we even correct at times: 'No, Demba, that's not the way it goes', and he replies: 'True, I forgot!' So Demba's stories are always really the same, but I pretend each time that I like them because Demba is so happy when we listen to him.

Sara sometimes wears the *melehva*, the immense veil, only she leaves her head, hair, arms, and all that exposed, nothing covering her, and it's very pretty, she musses her hair and smiles, and that, that does something to me right here, I say nothing but it does something to me, Momo claims that her hair is fake, I don't listen to him, because every time I talk about Sara he says something bad about her. One day we were playing hide-and-seek, and as I was running to find a hiding place and Sara saw me, and put a section of her veil over my head. 'There, I'll hide you!' She smelled good, I almost fainted I was so happy, and my head was close to her belly, her armpits, something even happened to me down below, I can't tell you, but Momo scolded me afterward: 'Don't hide beneath women again, it's not good', I didn't answer.

■ ■ ■

Mama had many kinds of perfume, beautiful small bottles sitting on her dresser, in many different colors, many shapes, small ones, tall ones, fat ones, and some that looked like women, Papa always said it was too much, that we were poor, and then he'd ask: 'How did you get these?' Mama would answer: 'My cousin has a big business, she goes to France and brings them back for me, she's rich, her husband is rich, and she lives well, she travels, not like me, and besides it's none of your business all this, it's women's stuff.'

Mama, I loved her very much but she was tough with Papa, she'd tell him he was poor, and she'd say over and over again that Malika was a name for a queen, that she had given her that name because a very, very long time ago there had been a Malika in her family who married a king who became very powerful and had taken her far away, she was a queen, she had everything, gold, soldiers, ministers, slaves. 'Not at all like me', she'd conclude, Papa wouldn't say anything, would even laugh about it sometimes, and when we were alone, I'd say: 'Mama, don't talk to Papa like that!' and she'd sneer at me: 'Ah, you're on his side now?' There wasn't anything else I could say.

There was a wedding the other day. Bahim's sister was married to one-eyed Dahi, yes, the shopkeeper. She came to do some shopping and he noticed how she'd grown, she has breasts now, and he told her mother: 'I want your daughter', the mother repeated this to her father, and that's how it happened. They set up two large tents in the street and huge cooking pots, and they put mats down and spent all day prepar-

ing the meal. At night everyone was there, the people in the neighborhood sang and danced the *bendja*, the dance we really like because the
women shake everything, their butt and their belly and everything.
We watched and we danced also, and we ate a lot, a whole lot, and
some people even took food home. Momo and I, we called Tenn and
Selma and Toto. 'Eat up,' we told them, and Selma filled her belly and
then said something from her behind that made us all laugh a lot.

But Bahim's sister didn't stay married for very long, it seems that
Dahi shouted from the rooftops that she wasn't a virgin, and so he di-
vorced her. Bahim said none of this was true, that his sister didn't like
the old man but Bahim is a liar and he doesn't know anything.

Milou is the biggest liar of all. We all know that he has no father,
but he, he claims that his father bought him a bike and he lends his
bike, but one day his mother came by and yelled at him: 'If you lend
it out, I won't buy you a bike again.' We didn't say anything in front of
her but when she left Saidou went: 'Is she your father?', we all laughed
and Milou wasn't very happy. Another day he said: 'My father left for
Mecca yesterday', we were very surprised. 'For Mecca? So your father,
he's rich?', he: 'Of course, he's a boss, my father', but later we told this
to Meimoune-who-sells-anything and he chuckled: 'Mecca, that's not
now, that's in three months.'

Me, they don't bother me anymore, thanks to Momo the kids of
PK7 leave my father and my mother in peace, if some kid says anything about my father or my mother, Momo breaks his face, even
Mokhis never says anything about me anymore. It's better now, but I
don't know anymore, thinking of 'it' makes me so sad and I feel like
crying, so I quickly run off to play with the children, that way I think
less, which is better.

Me, when I'm grown-up I'll work, I'll have a lot of money and

I'll marry Sara, that's for sure, one day I'll say to her: 'You see, Sara, me, I'm rich, I'm going to marry you, I'm still young now but that's no problem, I have money, I have everything, I'm going to marry you', and Sara who's very sweet, will say yes and we'll leave, no, we're not going to stay in PK7, we're going to leave, and Malika will be with us and Papa won't be in prison any longer, and Mama will have a beautiful grave, it will be fine, really fine.

THE FATHER

My darling,

All I want to remember today is this: our moments of joy. I want to erase the rest from my memory, eradicate what causes suffering, retain only those heavenly images where you clung to me, intoxicated on the beaches of bliss. Ecstatic, we'd lean over the crest of our pleasures and watch the display of the quivering skeleton of our past anxieties, way down below in the distance, broken-jointed and gaunt. Ah, how we laughed at our fears, how we ridiculed the ghosts that had haunted us, we believed ourselves to be the masters of our destiny. We thought we'd won, we were proclaiming victory, my love, because the moment blinded us. Ah, you see, in spite of myself they're coming back, those specters of our sorrows, suffering always keeps hanging on.

Never mind, I'm going back to what's joyful!

We escaped the very night of our wedding, we wiped away our tracks in the sand, and we fled. We took the northern route, all alone, we laughed loudly at the trick we'd played on the others, I was driving the sturdy car we'd rented at high speed, and you stuck out your head to inhale the air of a new life. 'Finally free,' you said. Today, my darling, I wonder: 'What is freedom?' but let's move on. I wanted to show you an idyllic spot, a lair for the lyricism of eyes and senses, a haven of love, the Banc d'Arguin, a place where the sea, the desert, and birds from every corner of the world meet up, a protected site, a refuge for migratory birds where we, too, could hide for a brief moment. After all, were we not migratory birds as well? The director of the place, a kind man in his forties whom one of my friends knew well, welcomed us warmly. A clean room where we spent a good part of our days. Maloum, the mute fisherman whose indistinct sign language made you laugh. We enjoyed the fresh fish and old Mame who was throwing her cowrie shells to promise us the most beautiful spring times and every night she'd tell us stories of another era. The days slipped past, we almost stayed too long.

But then we went back to be with the others, and you joyfully swept me into the midst of the dances of life, you finally wanted to get a taste of your desires, and fast, the dresses you hadn't been able to buy, the necklaces that no one had wanted to bestow upon you, the long nights of listening to the songs of the griots, the places where the poor are not allowed to go, the friends you wanted to impress, and I followed you everywhere, I wanted to feel close to you always, at every moment. Only—and you knew it—the places where you took me weren't mine, I felt like a stranger there and at times even quite preposterous, I couldn't understand at all what the pleasure might be in window-shopping, running from one store to another, spending an entire day gossiping in sad and stifling living rooms, listening to tasteless stories that never ended, inviting bad musicians to one's home. It's true, as you'd sometimes say, I don't know how to live, it's true, that despite all those years I continued to be a Bedouin, attached to his solitude, you certainly were aware of that. I was so unhappy when you'd laugh with the rest of them, when you'd open your arms to welcome them, when you'd try hard to be witty to please them. But our few hours of happiness made up for it all. And then our son was born.

■ ■ ■

It was your brother who sowed the first unrest in our heads. I knew that he didn't like me, but I thought that the birth of his nephew would bring us closer. He only became more horrible. He summoned me to your mother's house and in front of two witnesses he ordered me to sign a new marriage contract. 'I kept quiet at first to protect the honor of my little sister, but the first marriage was fake, the child who was just born was conceived out of wedlock, he's a bastard, he's simply a bastard, only the fear of a scandal has prevented me from repudiating him, so now you must return to what's lawful and to the path of God.' I didn't know what to say, I was ashamed and at the same time I felt it was an enormous injustice and above all I saw the contempt in his eyes, I've never been able to tolerate contempt in people's eyes. 'He is my son,' I replied in a voice that I tried to keep from shaking, 'he is my son, and she is my wife, and nobody can take them away from me.' 'You misled this little girl, you stole her, you made her pregnant so you could marry her, you know perfectly well that I would have never given her to you otherwise.' I had to control the horse that was kicking and neighing inside me, wanting to jump him. You'll ruin everything a voice told me, it's a ploy to deprive you of everything, to steal your loves. The two witnesses looked embarrassed and obviously wanted to move things along, one of them appealed to me: 'It won't cost you anything, my son, and it will remain a secret, your conscience will be better; God forgives, my son, when you know how to set things straight with him.' 'I have wronged no one,' I muttered faintly, then closed my eyes and signed, trembling with rage.

My darling,

What our son offered us was a different form of happiness, an immense delight. Do you remember how we'd lean over him, how we'd look at each other across his little cradle, how we'd wake up during the night when we heard him cry, the three of us we were a family.

We lived on a white cloud and didn't look around us, and then all of a sudden we found ourselves surrounded from all sides by the dreadful reality... and we discovered we were all alone and the world was watching us.

I have to stop writing because a huge racket has unsettled the prison. It's a high society gentleman who has come inside our walls, a wealthy man who has entered the jail of the excluded ones. The prisoners want nothing to do with him: 'Let him go back to those fancy cells for the big shots,' but, so the guards say, the problem is that he can't stay there, he doesn't have enough protection and his enemies can get to him more easily there. Well, a compromise was made, it was Ali who suggested the deal: the billionaire prisoner will pay rent, yes, each month he'll pay a sum of money, I don't know how much, and he can share our jail, the gang leaders will protect him here. And so peace returned. That's how a prosperous man of renown came to buy a bit of tranquility in an overpopulated prison. You know, my darling, everyone has their passions and all of them cause you to either live or die. This man, Ali explained to me, made a lot of money, he was in the fishing business, owned boats, traveled abroad, lived in beau-

tiful homes. Except that in his little village he was involved in politics, competing very heavily with his cousin, another rich man, who
wanted the support of the whole tribe just for him alone, he was filled
with hatred, with the rage of seeing the other one conquer hearts and
election ballots. Having turned crazy and blind, he sent his people to
assassinate his rival and so here he is, forced to find refuge with Ali
and his friends. You see where terrible passions can lead, my darling,
you see how crazy the world is not to know how to reconcile itself
around small things, a cup of tea, a walk outside in the fresh air, a
dune in the evening bathed in the light of the sky, a smile, your smile.

> *Dleim, Ghaylane, Mechdhouf*
> *Preferred wrath and want to stay with it*
> *Biyer, Sba, take a hard look,*
> *Saw the best among them fall*
> *And if only they'd seen a little girl*
> *Smiling, kneeling, reciting her first*
> *Alphabet letters*
> *All those tribes would reconcile around*
> *That tiny smile*

Do you recall who wrote that, it was our little game when we
were reciting poems. This time I won't lie to you: I don't know.

But I do remember very well that you'd laugh at me, at my fears
when our child sneezed, or when he cried for no reason, it's true,
you've always been strong.

Our funds ran dry, our fortune had gone up in smoke, we had
nothing left, I didn't dare go to my people, the bridges were burned,

and I didn't have the strength to show a change of heart, bow my head and ask forgiveness. Would they have even granted that to me?

And it's true, love of my life, that was hard for me, the shell of fine words that used to cover up my poverty burst open and I found myself as if naked before you.

■ ■ ■

My darling,

The nights have flown off, the beautiful days are buried under a thick burnous, the laughter that surrounded us has turned into scowls, our friendships into elusive, disdainful looks, penniless we were sent back to earth from our cloud, banned from the misleading stars that sparkled only for the blind, and you, you were grieving to see us so abandoned by everyone, but I didn't really care. I was actually almost happy over this reversal of fate, I had finally found my feet again and felt the earth beneath them, I told myself you would come back to me, you would forget the artificial dazzle, the sleazy friendships, you'd lean on my arm alone, and I would take you where we would only find our bliss, I told myself that all I had to do was work and we'd start a new life again without any commotion other than that of our own hearts, and we'd become a couple again like other couples, no, not like the others, because I loved you madly and that should certainly be enough.

I rented a not very large but comfortable house in PK7, a working-class neighborhood. It was my friend Moud who recommended it, it wasn't expensive, and above all it was far from the people we'd come to know and the universe we'd left, a get-away that I wanted to be permanent, burying the past, I would have you all to myself in an environment in which I'd know how to move, far from the fantasies that had stolen your heart, and I would teach you what true happiness is, stay together, feel strength in our back, our shoulders, our heart, drink and eat our fill, listen to simple poetry, the most melodious poetry that inhabits the heart. You didn't say a word, you looked at the house and I saw your tears roll down. I understood, cutting the umbilical cord that linked you to the false dreams was upsetting you, you were finally having to let go of your romance novels and your moronic soap operas, you were seeing your hopes for a crooning and carefree life founder. But I wasn't unhappy with those tears, they implied a defeat and maybe a victory for me, for I had a battle to fight, against me, against you, for the two of us and for our child who was already starting to run around; no, my darling, I wasn't afraid, I had confidence, I told myself that deep inside you something would be reborn and you'd know how to grasp it and create happiness from it, happiness is so simple, it's simply learning to sense the ordinary things that nourish every moment of the day.

Ah yes, it's true, I had to bow my head and admit everything, review for you the pitiful story of my boastfulness, rewrite the path of my madness and narrate it for you, but I wrapped it all up in the poetry of our tomorrows, I retraced the way I was going to embark on the plans that were waiting only for my willpower to become a reality; and for the Eden that in the end I would bring to bloom again at your feet, a veritable paradise, without any lies, and the sea spray that I would steal away from the beach and use to cover your body. I was going to switch gears, I knew it, into other inextricable nets, new chains, and the days were lying in wait to refute me but I told myself that to stay with me you needed starry horizons, you had to see distant signs of rain in order to accept being thirsty; and then maybe everything I promised you would ensue, one cannot disparage the goodness of God, he knows how to dispense his kindness without our expecting it as my people always said. Tomorrow you'll be able to forget everything, reconcile yourself with the sand and the walls of our new life, to change. Yes, that's all human beings are, images, words, resolutions that are forgotten, that's what we think down there of city dwellers, weak beings who are forgotten, who believe in their power while they are nothing, not even grains of sand in the middle of immense nature, less than trivialities, conceited and changing atoms. 'Whatever', you'd say again.

My friend Diallo is crying very softly, hiding his eyes behind his dark turban. The prisoners laugh about him. If he likes stealing those poor sheep that much, it's not just because of their meat, they say. He could do fine without his Raki and, in any case, there's no way she can love him, he has no teeth, he has no chin, his eyes are continually crusty, and he likes sheep too much. And every prisoner promises that once he's free he'll go and let sweet Raki know about the frenzy of the billy goat, deprived of fresh meat for so long. Diallo is crying very softly, I touch his back to calm him down, Ali doesn't come to his aid but laughs with the rest of them, the world in which I live now is not kind. But I know that Diallo will soon quiet down, then he'll laugh, and he'll tell us about Raki with the same passion, I envy Diallo, he manages to erase the light spots on a blackboard and write new letters that only he will know how to decipher.

Me too, I wanted to erase everything and build new words, I wanted to reconstruct our life with new bricks. I had no choice, the past didn't reach out to me, and I had to build our home of tomorrow on quicksand, for the two of us, the three of us, the four of us. You were expecting another child.

■ ■ ■

I wandered around for a long time to find a job in the public service arena and with companies, truth to tell I had nothing in my favor to present, no diploma, no life experience, nothing besides a fake smile I'd put on to show my good will, but that was clearly not sufficient. And then one day I passed a long line of slovenly people on the dole, mostly wearing filthy jackets and carrying crumpled papers. I joined the end of the line and patiently followed the slow progression of this lonely crowd that didn't even whisper, brooding over its inner agony and not wanting to break the charm of a hope that was, finally, perhaps a possibility: to find work and a little dignity. When my turn came, they asked for my papers but, in a language that had to be less coarse than that of the others, I simply mentioned the courses I'd studied and, above all, my wish to quickly obtain a place in the working world. I seemed to be persuasive because the red-headed gentleman who was watching me appeared to take an interest and the other, a Black man with a broad smile, asked me to come back the next day, I just had to produce a criminal record. They told me I'd be a foreman, which just required an internship of several months abroad, in a mine that the company owned in Africa.

I then considered dropping the whole thing, how could I be away from you for so long and how could I go so far away to a desert that had no nomads and no camels, in windswept shacks, sniffing the smell of huge cities, and not seeing you except on weekends or during an annual leave? My friend Moud cried: 'Have you gone mad, this is a godsend, God is reaching out his hand to you, you want to refuse the hand of God? You're crazy.' You threatened to leave me if I didn't accept. 'How would your continuous presence here with me help us live, how can the poems you sing to me at night buy me what I need, you think that loving is nothing but looking at me, you believe that our nightly embraces will provide milk for our son, clothes for me and, besides, you know perfectly well you have no family anymore, they've forgotten about you down there, time has nullified your bluster. What are you hiding behind? You think you don't need to work? It doesn't make any sense...'

The company for which I worked was a gold mine, an ore whose glitter I never felt, which left me only with calloused hands and blistered feet, all I knew was hard work, orders barked at me and that I sometimes barked as well, evenings when dead-tired I'd get to a clean shack where I lay down empty-headed, except for thoughts of you, where I'd talk to you across the distance and where in my dreams I'd see our son grow up and smooth out all the wrinkles of our life. At moments like that, it's true, when fatigue and boredom ate away at my spirit and senses, I could only see an escape by way of the future, the generation we would birth, our son who would make our final years flower again. And often, too, I admit, I would call on our old campsite, our pastures that were scarce, but so splendid to my eyes, our life of yesterday when I couldn't imagine any future other than the life I was leading, when the only concerns were those of nature, of diminishing grass, of rain slow in coming, a lost camel, the well drying up too quickly, the life of the Bedouins who see the sun come and go each day without ever questioning the logic of such restless wandering.

In the beginning the hardest thing was to leave you for three long months of internship far away in a rainy, humid country. I know that geography hardly counts among your worries, inside your head you merely want to draw the map of your desires, the world stops on the threshold of your will, and you're right not to want to make sense of today's world as I do. What did I achieve by reading newspapers, listening to the radio, being informed about the fate of a planet that forgets about us, about me and those I love, every day? You have always known how to situate things in relationship to yourself you don't lose yourself in the erudite twists and turns of this one and that one, you listen only to your heart, you shape your truth without ever turning back.

Oh, my darling, how hard they were, those days without you, I would often call you. 'Just don't call me all the time! All your savings will be spent on these phone calls', you'd answer. But what could I do? I needed to hear your voice.

■ ■ ■

It's raining today, drops of hesitant rain have formed small puddles of water in the courtyard: even prisoners have a right to the kindness of the sky. My heart always beats faster when the first splashes of rain arrive, I can't keep from thinking of the campsite, where they're taking down the tents, cries mingling all over the place, the animals are shackled, prayers mount as do the shouts of joy: winter rains are rare beneath our heavens, it's often said that they hardly promise a fine rainy season, but when they come everything's forgotten and the adults, hand shielding the forehead, look at the sky and predict the power of the rain. I'm hearing a prisoner sing rain's gentle, sad melodies, I forgot the words, they're words that evoke the mellow, sweet sound of drops kissing the sand, that carry the nostalgia of lovely pastures and the fear of tomorrow, yes, despite everything rain means anxiety, it heralds wild and vague tomorrows, floods that will carry people off, trees that may perish, travelers who will lose their way but, come what may, the rain is always welcome, whatever it destroys in the end it restores everything, at least that's what they say where I'm from.

When I was far away in the land where the rain never stops, I would be surprised at the persistence, the mess, the madness. I did once read you, my darling, the story told in a famous book by a well-known writer who loves the desert and the Sahara: men from our area who were invited to Paris early in the twentieth century, who were not impressed by the Eiffel Tower, or by the Invalides, or by the huge buildings, but only by the first fountain they encountered; they stopped in front of this unimaginable, magical display, waiting patiently for the good Lord to finally put an end to this folly. I felt they must have looked around and been astonished at this foolishness: so much water, so much greenery, and not a camel in sight, no tent, no date palm, no dune, what a waste! Had the world fallen apart?

Ah, true, my darling, I generalize but, remember, you used to really appreciate my digressions.

You know, my darling, it ripped me apart when I found the place where I was going to work. It was one of our pasture lands, it's where we took our animals to graze in years when the rainy seasons were good, my brother would cite you the name of every one of the dunes that appear so similar. They didn't know that Tasiast was sacred land during years when the rains were good, when the grass was at its most nutritious for the camels, and when a wind comes from very far off, from the distant shores of the Atlantic, and caresses the heads of us children. No, they didn't know anything, and their huge equipment came to eviscerate the earth and their rumbling machines came to disrupt the ancient serenity of the place, they didn't know that every little corner of the desert was thoroughly familiar with the period when it eagerly welcomed us, and that this was all inscribed in the heart and spirit of the people. There's a time for tents to be raised and a time when the earth is to be left alone, there's a time for everything. They had no clue, nothing, they didn't understand life's eternal calendar, they had compasses, clocks, talking computers, telephones that crisscross the sky, but they had no idea of how to listen to the sand's murmuring, of the Sahara's truth that would inevitably cover everything, they camped indefinitely in the same space, they tormented the earth and the dunes that were listening to them, and they thought that thereby they could seize the wind's inviolable secrets. They were just ignorant, after all.

How hard they were, those days without you, the relentless labor, the screaming machines, the bad smells, the body that turns completely senseless and makes movements without thinking, words that as a result of constant repetition became merely sounds, stripped of any delight, grunts bereft of meaning, and the enormous, insolent scrapheap that saw itself as sovereign over a land without a master. But I swear to you, inside this holy hell swarming with howling machinery and wordless ennui, I was thinking of you, I'd hear your voice, I'd see your smile, and I'd dream of our child running across the sand dunes.

However, I have to admit that, despite your advice and your reprimands, I wasn't able to silence the turmoil inside me. Truthfully, I didn't have the courage to resist the confidence my friends in the mine had shown in me. I soon became the most prominent trade unionist, not that my values were any greater than theirs, not that I was more committed to the interests of the workers, but quite simply because I knew how to write a text, understand labor laws, speak the language of the managers and, anyway, that sort of camaraderie pleased me, I found a little of myself getting back in it, I found a family there, oh I know, it's not really family, but I didn't feel so alone in the face of that headless monster, having arrived from some far-flung place. We found out that it was everywhere, in innumerable countries and with innumerable people, it didn't have a country or a people of its own, it was feeding everywhere on land wherever it would find any, on the intelligence of the people and of their arms, its pulse would beat at the rhythm of incomprehensible numbers displayed on fluorescent screens that thousands of people would watch with wide-open mouths, their bellies always wanting new sustenance even though they were already full.

I should also say that it helped me to endure the long weeks without you. With ever more feverish impatience I'd await the days of freedom when I would run toward you. I'd jump into the first available truck, my head filled with the joys in store for me.

True, each time I came back you'd complain a little because I wasn't bringing enough money, because the district seemed too poor in your eyes, because you didn't care for the neighbors, because you couldn't 'properly' receive any friends, only some relatives or your brother's wife. Exhausted from three weeks of hard work, I almost never went out, I spent the day playing with our child and conquering you, yes, every time I came back, I had to vanquish you again, rekindle a fire whose flames I sensed were gradually extinguishing inside you.

How lonely I would feel at times, watching humanity live through the windows of my solitude. My only relationship with the world was through you or through the mine. My former friends had taken different paths, they had gone abroad or chosen the civil service. In any case, the course our lives we were following was too dissimilar, I, the 'petty bourgeois', the 'defeatist', I had become a laborer, while they, the 'activists of the cause', had embraced wonderful careers. And I didn't have the courage either to renew the ties with our campsites, I didn't even know where they were anymore. Perhaps they had chosen distant lands, perhaps they had finally settled on the edge of a city, neither urban dwellers nor truly nomads, breathing in the scents of the great outdoors without actually answering the calls of the vast sands. I had broken with everything that formed my past, in spite of myself.

■ ■ ■

I hear loud shouting, angry rumbling.... It's been a few hours since I was able to be alone and finally get to write to you again.

There was a fire in the prison, they'd lit four corners of the courtyard, taken out knives and blades, refused to let the guards come in. They were bellowing loudly, some had scaled the walls and were on the roof waving their shirts like so many flags of rebellion.

They were demonstrating in support of my friend Ali, demanding that he be released. He had served his sentence, but the authorities were balking at liberating an incarcerated man who had obviously benefited from the too-great leniency of a judge. He himself wasn't present at the rebellion that he had clearly fomented, he was sitting calmly beside Diallo, watching the jailers' unease with a smirk, he wasn't going to give them any reason to extend his detention; he's the terrible hand that shakes the seeds in the sieve of decline, the hand that only carries out the most serious felonies and then rises to swear to his innocence. I really have to admire him a little, on his face I see the tension of anxiety, of pride, the moments of fear, then at last the satisfied smile when he hears that the authorities agree to negotiate. I imagine this man in politics, in religion, in the military, what a leader he would be to us, greeted or loathed by the crowds, but Ali didn't choose that path, he's a thief, period, that's it; a delinquent, maybe a criminal, and the signs of doom show on his face. This man is committed to violence, today he delights in it, tomorrow he'll die of it, but I don't think for a moment that he's unhappy, I don't think for a moment that he's groping in the void, roaming around his conscience to look for a lost truth, his truth is inside him, always: he doesn't even need to formulate his profound contempt for human conventions, his truth isn't expressed, it's a feeling, it always lies dormant deep inside him and all it takes is a harsh look, a derisive smile, sparks lighting up inside his heart, for the sacred and senseless rage to be reborn.

He is relishing his victory now, lying down with his hands behind his head, a cigarette in his mouth, raising his torso from time to time to listen to a prisoner give his report, he's a leader, he's real, he's tough, as he likes to call himself.

How many times did you blame me for not having any steel inside me, only weakness when confronted with things, negligence in the face of life's demands, you would describe people for me I wasn't familiar with, serious people who'd become rich, they were in business you'd say, they had connections you'd say, they knew how to cut and paste things, as you put it, they flanked important people and profit from it, they were involved in politics and in a lot of other things, you'd add, as if to make me guess at what lay underneath the real battle that these heartless knights were capable of waging. I didn't really understand what you wanted me to be, I never learned how to approach others for no reason, I never learned how to lean against a tree whose foliage wasn't meant for me, I was always getting lost in the labyrinths where I hadn't been invited, I only knew how to navigate in the great desert, close to my people, or operate thanks to my muscles, to my mind, to what belonged to me.

Malika was born without our being aware of the distance that separated us from then on. Or perhaps we were! I knew you were moving away from me but I refused to admit it, I knew you were looking elsewhere but I couldn't find the direction you were looking for. Of course, my love, of course it's all my fault. I know that now. I will never accuse you of anything, never again will I toss the rotten fruits of my gloomy condition in the basket gleaming with lovely things that you've carried off with you.

I was very well aware that you had forged new friendships, your phone wouldn't stop ringing and, incensed at my presence, at my suspicious looks, you'd grumble and hang up; I never said anything, I was only trying to have us reconnect, to bring the sap back to the weakened branches, you'd give yourself to me but you were somewhere else, I felt it very clearly, fuming inside, kicking myself inside, I was screaming in silence, but to whom could I have complained?

Our children, I surely tried to hold you by those strings, but please don't think for a moment that I was using them, no, I love them deeply, you know that very well, I watched over them when they had a fever and you were asleep, I'd get up late in the night to pamper them and not disrupt your sleep, I'd run with them, I played, I clowned around, and I was happy when sometimes you'd join us and when you'd say on the verge of tears: 'You're nothing but a child yourself', yes, I'm just a child, love of my life, I'm just a young boy frantically running after a lost ball that, etched in its leather, bears the signs of a madness buried beneath the trash of the new cities.

They're going to turn off the lights, soon you will appear to me in the brightness of the night.

THE SON

I like the morning when nobody's around, when the earth and people are silent, I slip out onto the streets and often spread my arms wide, like this, our PK7 closes its eyes, the world is still asleep and stays soundless, it's dark and yet the sky is growing lighter, just a little so as not to brighten things too much, and me, I say: Papa and Mama are here, very nearby, they're going to come on this day that hasn't awakened yet, they're just asleep and everything will get up at the same time, when the Muezzin calls, now, everything will wake up, the past, Mama, Papa, and we'll all go off together with little Malika, because it's not normal that everything's been stolen from us, it's not normal, and this morning everything will wake up.... Yes, that's how I think. Sometimes I'm just crazy, I swear.

And yet, every day I repeat to myself: Don't think about it, it's too awful, don't think about it. But I can't stop myself, Papa, Mama, Malika, they're here inside my head, and even when we're playing sometimes it comes back, and even when I'm sleeping sometimes it comes back, it won't let go of me, I swear.

In our PK7 they never come to empty the garbage cans. Even the government people finally said: 'There's too much trash at the PK, it's filthy, it causes disease...' Meimoune-who-sells-anything told us that the President-on-the-photograph saw it on television, that it made him angry, and that he gave the order to have everything cleaned up. So, one day huge trucks arrived with people in them who had wheelbarrows and shovels, and the men in our neighborhood worked with them, too, even Mokhis' father, and then they told us children: 'You should help your district, if you cart all that filth to the same place, we'll give you something.' So we left, it was easy, there were plenty of garbage cans everywhere, they lent us wheelbarrows, we filled them, we took them to the huge container and the big truck picked it all up, and then that evening some guy handed us coins, very little, one small coin a piece, that's all, nothing really but we're smarter than that. At night when they were leaving, we brought the cart of Messaoud's father, we loaded it with part of the remaining trash, which we hid behind a wall nearby, then we picked it up the next morning and took it to the truck and they gave us some more change. They gave very little so we didn't wear ourselves out and there wasn't anything they could do with all those trashcans there and the orders from the President-on-the-photograph. So they continued and we continued until the day that we didn't see them anymore. There were still trashcans left, of course, and Momo laughed. 'They don't know it, they don't know that it's us, we're the trash', there are kids who don't like to hear us say that but Momo is the leader, he can say whatever he wants.

Papis goes to school, you know, because his father is a guard there, so he has to go, even if it means that he has to sweep the classroom in the morning and that the teacher tells him: 'Sit in the back.' He's always at the back of the room, Papis, because he's dirty and he doesn't always return after recreation time, and he knows nothing, even we know more than he does. Still, he's our friend no matter what, even if he's ashamed that he's still going to school, but Momo told him: 'It's no problem, you're an ass anyway', then we all laughed, even Papis.

Momo isn't really here anymore, always at his garage and he doesn't come home until evening, and when he comes home he listens to the radio and claims he's tired, he's got a lot of work, he carries heavy loads on his back for the customers, he slides down under cars. His boss doesn't kid around, and his father goes over there every day to make sure he's working hard. Sometimes I go to see him at the garage as well, I sit down on a black bench and Momo brings me bread and tea and now and then he gives me a coin or two, and I see the other apprentices, they're very young, there's even one who's my age, and they don't talk, they don't play, they just work, that's all, even if they're puny, poor kids, and the boss slaps them at times. But it's Momo who lugs the heavy loads. Even though his boss is always yelling at him and insulting him, Momo never says anything, he really has become a man, one day he'll be a fulltime mechanic, that's for sure.

Sara now always talks with Momo when she walks by. Each time Momo shows up: 'Hello, Sara', and Sara stops: 'Hello, Momo', and they chat a little, I let them, I say nothing, just 'Hello, Sara', then Sara puts her hand on my head, 'Everything alright, my brother?', and I say yes and walk along with her a little way and sometimes she gives me fritters, cookies, things like that, and later I say to Momo: 'You see, Sara gave me this, she's sweet', he no longer tells me she's insolent and such, he says nothing, only: 'I see, I see.'

Mokhis has become the leader, or that's what he decided anyway and the others agree because Momo's always at his garage. Me, I don't speak, I don't say anything, I don't even want to hang out with the kids any longer, it makes no sense because I know that Momo will always be the real leader.

■ ■ ■

I heard father Moud speak about Papa, he was talking to mother Maria and thought I couldn't hear, he was saying that Papa was basically a good man, that he was just unhappy, but that he was good in spite of it all. Mother Maria asked: 'What did he say in the courtroom?' According to father Moud, Papa claimed he'd gone crazy, that he was sorry, and that he'd accept any decision the judge would make. Mother Maria asked God to forgive Mama, for me it was as if I'd been hit on my head, I wanted to ask what is a courtroom, what is a judge, and I wanted to say that all of this was wrong, that what the kids say when they're at war with me is wrong: Mama didn't do anything and Papa didn't do anything against Mama, and he's in there only for a short while. But I was afraid of father Moud, he doesn't like kids listening at the door, that's what he always says.

Sometimes, I swear, I'm not myself anymore, I say that my family is rich, that our house is large, that there's plenty of everything, food, games, even cars, I hand money out to the PK7 kids, even to Saidou: 'Here, take it, it's okay!' and to Momo I say: 'Come, you're my friend!' and to father Moud and mother Maria: 'You're like my parents, and you're going to live very well because we are rich.' Mama is there, and Papa, too, he's smoking very fancy cigarettes, and Malika has a nanny who does nothing else but take care of her, and I have shoes and nice clothes, and for a few minutes it's as if it was true, and I even talk out loud to say to the houseboys: 'Bring all that fine food and then turn on the big TV!' and Sara looks at me and I look at her, and I forget everything, I swear, I dive deep down in that dream and then I wake up and look around. Nothing there. And I want to cry! It isn't good to dream too much.

■ ■ ■

Momo has turned into a good man. Every day he brings something home from the garage, money and also things he always hides in his cash box. He has a big, strong steel box now and the children can't touch it, not even Selma, not even Toto, it's not allowed, but I know that he collects car parts and then sometimes, at night or on Fridays, he sells them. Momo is a grown-up now, and he gives me some money every day, and I buy stuff, and don't give my dues to Mokhis anymore.

Mokhis repeats it every day: 'We're collecting dues!' and the kids give him a coin, for a ball or a soccer jersey or some other thing, and later nothing's delivered. One day I had nothing and I told Momo: 'I have nothing to pay dues with.' Momo asked me: 'What dues?', so I told him and he went off to see Mokhis and handled him like a thief, a crook, and even like someone corrupt, as father Moud always says. Since then Mokhis doesn't ask me for any dues anymore, but I'm the only one who gets a pass.

Momo has almost become a boss, he even said he was going to buy an old motorbike and that Selma and I and even Toto could get on the back. 'I can do repairs all on my own now,' he said, 'and my boss pays me.' And also: 'The kids of the PK, they're just nobodies!'

He's almost a boss and he wears clean clothes and he goes out to see girls. Me, I'm waiting—when I'm bigger I'll be just like him.

■ ■ ■

After 'it', a month or almost a month after 'it', my uncle-my-father's-brother showed up, he was traveling, he'd found things out for Papa, and he came to pick me up. Father Moud tried very hard: 'Leave him with us for now!', but my uncle-my-father's-brother answered: 'No, he has to leave, his home is down there.' And he added: 'If his father had stayed there, things would have been better!' Father Moud put all my clothes in a bag and mother Maria gave us plenty of cakes and we left, first we took a huge truck, we were way on top, and I saw the dunes and the trees rush by, then the truck stopped and we got off, just the two of us, we stayed in a place, I couldn't see anything, it was completely dark, I swear, and the truck left, and the two of us were alone, not a sound, I swear, and my uncle-my-father's-brother put a blanket down on top of the dune: 'We'll sleep here until tomorrow!' Me, I didn't sleep, I was looking around everywhere, I was scared, I imagined 'djinns', I heard the wind weep, the moon disappeared behind the clouds for a long time, then it came out again, a tiny light, it left again, in the distance I heard a noise, the lion? I woke up my uncle: 'It's the lion.' 'Go to sleep, there's no lion here, there's nothing; go to sleep!' and I kept straining my ear again, but this time nothing, I fell asleep, I don't know when.

When I woke up, my uncle-my-father's-brother was praying. 'You pray, too!' I obeyed, it had been a long time, I'd even forgotten the words, but I muttered under my breath, my uncle-my-father's-brother didn't pay any attention, then a camel arrived" and another one behind him, I didn't get it at first, but the second camel was our car with a high seat on top, and my uncle-my-father's-brother put me on it, I was afraid, I yelled, but he sat down behind me and held on to me, and he had a rope to lead with, suddenly I was less afraid. The camel stood up making 'brrr' sounds, the dust flew up and I yelled again, but my uncle-my-father's-brother laughed: 'It's nothing, it's nothing'; then it was as if we were on top of a truck, we were barely balanced but we didn't fall off, and the dunes didn't rush by, and our shadow was large like in creepy films and me, I said to myself: maybe this isn't me, there's no Mama, there's no Papa, no Malika, no house, no PK7, just camels, maybe this isn't me! Me, I swear, sometimes I'm really stupid.

When we arrived, I couldn't believe my eyes. All I saw were scattered tents, I thought: This isn't it, but it was, and my uncle-my-father's-brother shouted something at the camel who sat down as if he were falling, in front of a tent, and a fat woman came out with a little child who was even dirtier than the kids of PK7, and she said to me: 'You okay? You're now like my son!' I was going to answer that I was only Mama's son but she was fat and she had big eyes. Then I ate old couscous and had some milk, and then I slept, I was so tired.

It was hard, all of this was hard, they woke me up in the morning, very early in the morning, you could still see the stars in the sky, yes, stars and they wanted to sleep like us, the stars closed their eyes, then they left to go to sleep; we lit a big fire and we read the Koran on our small wooden tablets, and the teacher, who had a huge beard, had a whip and kept turning around and around us and had us repeat the words of the Koran. When we were wrong, crack, he'd hit you very hard on the back, sometimes you didn't even see it coming, 'crack!' on the back or the head, and you'd cry a little and keep going, shouldn't make any mistakes, there was one who was always making mistakes and the teacher was always hitting him, poor kid, but it seemed that it didn't bother him, he kept on making mistakes.

After the Koran came the well, yes, we're going to get water; you think it was a faucet or like at the PK7, the public fountain where we stand in line? No, we're going to the well, which is very far, we have to walk a long way, behind the donkey who carries the goatskins and, when we get there, there are often camels, lots of camels, and their owners don't kid around, you can't take their place, they say they have far to go, they go first, that's it. So we wait and after- wards we draw water, it's way down the well, the water is, believe me, we toss a big bag like this on a long rope, and we wait until it's full, and then all together we pull it up. We pour it in the goatskin, throw the bag back down, pour it in the goatskin, and there's the sun smacking your head, once it was as if I was almost dead, I fell, I couldn't see anything anymore, I'd fainted. They said: 'It's nothing, it's the sun', they spent a lot of time wash-ing my head, they took me to the tent and put henna on me; that's how it works, no hospital, nothing, just henna, that's how it goes down there. So we fill the goatskins, we put them on the donkey, and we go home, and then it's back to the Koran and we don't get to play until after the Koran. They don't know how to play games, Bedouins, they throw stones on stones or they tell riddles, they don't know anything, there's no TV, no Play; we eat, their food is no good, no tomatoes, no potatoes, no fish, just meat and rice or corn or barley, and couscous and milk at night, always milk and meat, I was getting sick of milk and meat. And then my uncle's wife, I always heard her say to people: 'His mother, she was just trash', and she said other things about Mama that I can't repeat, and then one day I screamed: 'That's a lie! That's a lie!' She was mad, she insulted my mother, I kept saying: 'That's a lie, you're lying!' and when my my father's brother came, she told him. He didn't speak to me, but I heard him say: 'You've got to understand, he was at PK7, in the city, there, they know nothing there, you've got to give him time, it'll pass.' I didn't agree but I kept quiet.

Actually, I was tired, I swear, tired of the desert, the camels, the well, and my uncle's wife, I wanted to go see Malika, and visit where Mama was and where Papa's prison was. Maybe Papa has even come out of prison, that's what I told myself deep down inside.

And one day I got sick, oh yes, I was throwing up a lot, so my uncle decided: 'We're going to leave to see the doctors in the city,' and we took the camel, then the truck, we went into the city, we visited the clinic and they gave me a shot, ouch, it wasn't fun, but anyway I didn't cry, then we went to the market to shop for the tents and for a pair of pants for me. And then, while my uncle was talking with a vendor, I split; at first, I ran, then I asked: 'Where is PK7?' and they told me, so I ran again. I went back to the house, father Moud was glad and Momo, too, and little Selma yelled: 'Ichou!' and Toto danced for me. But I knew that my uncle would come and get me, that was for sure, so Momo hid me in an old shack where nobody lived anymore. He brought me water and peanuts and bread. My uncle looked for me everywhere, with father Moud's help even, but they didn't find me. Momo would say: 'I dunno', and two days later my uncle got the point and left things with father Moud and told him: 'I leave him in your hands now.'

I stayed at PK7, I was done with the desert and the well and the Koranic teacher, I was fine.

THE FATHER

I dreamed of you, my destiny, in my dream I saw you dancing in the middle of a circle of men who were applauding you, they seemed frozen, dead, only their hands were moving, and they all had the same face, the same hideous smile revealing totally black canine teeth, and they were wearing dark suits underneath very white boubous and instead of a tie they had attached a piece of hemp, and their shoes were camel's hooves, every now and then they'd shiver, all at the same time in the same motion as if the cold had suddenly frozen them; I was watching from afar, from the top of a high mountain, I was waving my arms and crying: 'Don't get near them, my love, they're djinns, they will chew up your heart, they will crush your soul', my call came echoing back but you, you didn't hear me, you kept dancing, deaf and mute, without looking around, and you were turning ceaselessly in the middle of these sharp-toothed phantoms. I was afraid of losing you, my love, of seeing you ripped to shreds by these monsters, so I leapt down from the mountain toward you. That's when I woke up in a sweat.

Ah, how lucky it would have been if the dream were real, for I would have known how to defeat even the djinns and get you back again, I wouldn't be here in the middle of nothing waiting for nothing, I would be close to you, and perhaps we'd be alone together, like the couple of Bedouins we met once in the heart of the Tiris region, do you remember?

We'd left to join one of my friends who was going on a family vacation and had invited us to his wedding there. We got lost in the middle of an ocean of sand. I'd made sure to get directions, I had made note of the mileage, the roads, the wrong tracks to avoid, the landscapes we'd see and, besides, I prided myself on being the son of golden spaces, on having the geography of the sands etched on my genes. But the desert always abandons us when we aren't humble. As we turned around a high dune, I suddenly found myself in an unfamiliar place.

I had no idea where we were anymore, for almost two hours we were going around in circles without being able to locate ourselves on this immense map of silent nature. Neither the stones, nor the dunes, nor the rare dying grass would speak to us, the sun seemed to want to devour us, and the sand was already growing impatient to embrace us in its folds; I no longer had a clue of what route I'd taken or which one I needed to head for, you were cursing my recklessness, sniveling that you could already see us dying of thirst in the vast barrenness, and I was gritting my teeth, suffering as much from your distress as from the fear that began to grow inside me; then all of a sudden we saw a tent appear in the distance, pitched on top of a dune all by itself, far removed from anything else. The big car I'd rented struggled to follow the movement of my eyes which kept watching the outstretched hand, I refused to avoid any obstacles so I wouldn't lose sight of the tent while you were wailing now about the bumps I made you endure.

In the tent we found a smiling young woman, carelessly wearing a dark veil that left her round shoulders and long hair uncovered. She slowly came forward to greet us, welcoming us with great kindness, a saving angel coming to call us back into the world. The tent was wide, the furniture simple, long relatively clean mats, white sheepskins gleaming in the sun's reflection, a camel saddle in a corner, a few embroidered cushions, a huge trunk in the back. A baby was sleeping in another corner, naked, its fists tightly closed. She refused to listen to us when we gasped a few vague questions. 'No, no, first you rest up, don't ask any directions too soon, that brings bad luck.' She immediately offered us some *zrig*, a thirst-quenching mixture of water and camel's milk, and then began to make tea. Still disoriented from our misadventure, we didn't say a word but began to wonder about the presence of this young woman all alone in the middle of nowhere, when we saw a man with a turban on a camel rounding the corner of a dune; he headed in our direction and with a loud cry made the animal kneel down. He was surprisingly slender, wore a boubou that came down to his knees and baggy white trousers no higher than his thighs. Right away, we noticed the flash of joy illuminating the young woman's face and the smile the camel driver gave her before he came to welcome us. Then he disappeared for a moment before returning to speak with us. They had left their campsite, some miles away, for a few days and chosen this place because measles were spreading there and they wanted to protect their baby from any contamination. 'And besides,' he added surreptitiously caressing her with his eyes, 'we also wanted to get away a little, be alone together, just the two of us.' She stood up and the man stayed to continue talking with us, they offered us a lamb tajine that you thoroughly enjoyed and a glass of refreshing tea. Then the man got up to show us which road to take; his directions were clear, he spoke in a calm voice as he watched me to make sure I understood. 'I was born in the desert,' I said to reassure him, which got me a nice smile and a handshake. We had no further trouble orienting ourselves. For a long time afterward we would bring up that encounter, those two people living far from everything, completely unaware of today's commodities, who seemed so happy to be together, perhaps not realizing their happiness because they were immersed in it at every moment, I expressed my amazement to you at the frenzy for objects that overtakes people, that craze for things, that race to the inaccessible. 'They always want more, when being happy is so simple, after all, when loving each other and not suffering is enough.' You pouted at my reflections because you had no answer and you were buckling under the whirlwind of things.

Were we made for one another? A strange question really. And yet, you often asked that of yourself, especially toward the end. I pretended not to hear because I refused to see the cracks, all I saw was a wall, a bulwark against the ferocities from outside, which I wanted to build with you no matter what the cost. And then, are there truly any people who are made for one another? Still, you believed it, you'd repeat the verse lines:

> *In the firmament up high*
> *It was written that I would love you*
> *It was written that I would touch your hand*
> *It had been said already*
> *The poem I say for you now*
> *And my suffering, too, was inscribed up high*
> *So what could I have possibly done?*

It was written in the stars: I have no destiny other than you.

I don't believe that poet, no, people are absolutely not predestined for love. It's a battle, it's a fight to the death, it's raids that first call us and defer to our primary being. True, animals fight, ancient tribes fight, children fight, countries wage war, in reality love is not an ordinary feeling, it's a happy aberration, a seed that surfaces in us, carried by unfamiliar, far-flung winds. You see, love of my life, it's still what you would call 'nonsense'.

Imagine, my love, the newspapers are mentioning me. For the first time I saw my photo in the press, I had my head down, my eyes lowered, my hair disheveled, a true crook, one could say. It's an identity picture, the photo from my work card. Who gave it to them? The comments range from criminal act to insanity. I'm described as a failure, an eternal loser, a bloodthirsty violent man. No, you know that's not who I am. If you were still here, you would have attested to that.

You know, carefully buried here under my pillow, I have a picture of you, laughing heartily, your head raised looking as if it wants to greet the sky, and your chest pointing forward as if it seeks to cling to me, I took that photograph on the beach, when we were getting away from the city, the noise, the awful smells and from people, to taste the offerings of the sea and the wide-open spaces far from everything else.

I stopped writing for a moment, the noise here is deafening, I can't even hear myself think anymore. The prisoners are celebrating their victory. They're shouting, dancing, Diallo is this party's grand organizer, he's the one wiggling about encircled by the crowd's applause, he steals, I know, ungodly hours of joy from the time that will not pass, he doesn't even hear the sarcastic comments from some of the prisoners yelling 'Raki, Raki!' and holding their penises, he continues to spin with the sides of his boubou in the air, oh, I know it well, the dance Diallo so clumsily performs; it's *Lebleida*, the dance of delights and devotions, it shouldn't be performed like this, it requires concentration, head up high, fingertips and body swaying gently, moving forward gracefully without seeming to move, as if not perceiving what's around you, it's only beautiful women who excel in this, not Diallo, oaf that he is.

Ali is leaving the prison tomorrow, he'll join the brightness of day, for a few months, perhaps a few short years, before he'll be back in here, the dark side of his fate. I don't pity him, his life is full, it's chosen a path and follows it in its ramblings, its stampedes, its torrents, he doesn't give himself a shoal on which to run aground, yes, maybe I ought to envy him.

Me, I've never managed to reach the shores of which I was dreaming. I wanted to go where you were, you and the children, bathe each day in the quiet serenity of peaceful moments, be comfortable with everyday language, with the habits of every moment, the laughter, the spats, the small joys and small troubles, that's all I asked for, the bliss of modest people, and I never even had that.

Yes, it's all my fault, I couldn't abide the men who surrounded you, I couldn't stand the phone calls you received, the cigarette butts I'd find in the ashtray or tossed out the window, the clothes and jewelry you wore that were too expensive for our budget, and that distant look, that absence in you that I would see. You no longer loved me.

I should have begged you on my knees to come back to me, to take me back again into your heart and your thoughts. But foolish pride prevented me. Essentially, I'm quite sure today that I didn't deserve you, I should have squelched all my stupid pride that kept me from bowing down before you even more, from licking the ground beneath your feet, from thanking heaven for having you by my side, it's true, I failed, but perhaps my shattered heart deserves a little pity, too.

Yes, I sensed it, you were already in a different place, during our last months you were already far away, I felt the brilliance of the smiles no longer meant for me ebb away between my fingers, I felt that your arms no longer responded to mine, your body drifting elsewhere when I embraced you and clouds of regret surreptitiously moving across your eyes. But what could I really do against shadows? I refused to question the signs, I was afraid of the words that risked emerging from the still mute opacity of things and striking me down, me who was, I thought, wholly innocent.

Our son would sometimes mention certain uncles whom I didn't know he had, certain neighbors would make vague allusions whose meaning I didn't want to interpret, and during my all too short home leaves I was too much of a fool to pay attention to anything besides you and the children.

That night—I don't think I really remember it—everything was dark inside my head, before my eyes, rage was blinding me, while I also felt a heavy ache in my abdomen. Madness had exploded inside me, a storm was crashing through all the barriers that the mind had put up, I myself had become that insane, avenging hurricane, and I believe that I was screaming words that had been stripped of their meaning, that made no sense because my wits had forsaken me, all I'd glimpsed was that shadow that had fled and you, naked and already imploring, I'd seen you depart, vanish, leave me forever. I think I grasped you forcefully by the throat and roared my refusal at being abandoned, I strangled you they said, no, I was kissing you, I was holding you back with all my strength, I was wrenching you away from the vicious invaders who'd come to trample our pastures, I wanted to pull from inside you what belonged to me and see the mire that had been meandering around for much too long drain far, far away, I heard nothing, not even your slow dying under my hands, not the sobs of my children, not the clamor of the neighbors who'd finally called the police and broken down the door to enter. I was excruciatingly alone facing the giants of dark lands with whom I had to do battle to remain myself and regain you, I fought them off when they came to tear me away from you, I wanted to die with my head between your breasts.

It's too hard, my darling, I'm going to stop writing.

It's ridiculous, but I thought I could hide my tears from you. But there where you are, you can see anything. True, I still cannot get used to your absence. There are moments when I imagine myself elsewhere and you're going to come join me, and I will hear our children laugh, and sometimes I tell myself that this isn't me, here inside this jail, slumped on a mattress gnawed at by mold and time, surrounded by wretched men who've lost everything and have chosen to be lost, no, this cannot be me, I could only live two kinds of life. Down there, in my native Amessaga, amidst our rare grass and our lands that are white from having endured it all, or close to you who do not know how to assume a burden. There is no other life, and I often hear something that sounds like a call, I tell myself it's you: 'But where are you now?' it's always with this question that your calls begin.

In spite of all the prohibitions, almost all the prisoners here have a cell phone, I don't. Whom would I call? You, my darling, are off the network, as they say, you cannot be reached, you live where only hearts communicate. I know, I could have not written these letters, it's true, it's as it is with words, they don't express everything, sometimes they distort, they don't get to what's real, letters float in the air and don't adhere to bodies, or hearts, or minds, they hover above what's living but don't penetrate it, words are lies, like life. Me, I need them because I'm helpless, I'm scared of what surrounds me and of myself, I escape my prison and refuse to think of the things I've lost, of our abandoned children. Perhaps I shouldn't have written all this, perhaps the words will feel betrayed and won't echo inside me anymore, won't accept not hiding anything anymore. So what? Let the words go away if that's what they want.

Diallo is crying. He says he wants to die, he's insulting the female gender, beating his chest and shaking his head, he takes me as a witness for his heart that has always been ablaze for his lady-love and that despair will extinguish today. She has married, and whom? An unimportant carter, he yells. The prisoners laugh. 'That's because you have too many mistresses, Diallo, and she sometimes hears them bleat at night,' 'It's nothing, women run the streets, Diallo, as for behinds, even goats have them.' The entire prison sniggers and Diallo protests. These morons keep making fun of this simple-minded man. I try to console him, but I know that wounds are quite deaf to caresses, that they bow only to time, and that always runs through our fingers.

Ali is leaving prison today, he got nicely dressed for the occasion. His boubou is made of precious, immaculately white bazin, his shirt looks as if it came straight from a shop in Paris, his pants are of the finest quality. He walks around like a mogul among the ragged prisoners who're watching him, he's waiting for the hour of deliverance, he's not impatient, he should have gotten dressed once he was outside but the supervisors let him do what he wanted. Who will replace Ali? Will the prisoners manage to agree on a new leader? No, I don't think so. Several gang leaders will share the power, even if they have to confront each other despite the steel bars that separate them, that's the tough law of life, the merciless logic of the balance of power, the one that animals and children are all too familiar with, and that adults pretend to ignore. 'Whatever,' you would have said, yes, you'd be right: whatever, the laws that guide us, are whatever!

It's my brother who told me this: our son is back at PK7. He ran away to go back to the dark streets of our modest neighborhood. I really cannot hold it against him. Life in the desert is hard for a child who's known nothing other than the overcrowding of poor districts. The peacefulness of the days there rends the vibrating madness of today's cities where silence is unbearable, this relief assaults with its clarity, boredom or what one believes to be boredom sets in, and that is only the anguish of seeing the world in its own truth, uncovered, without any dirty sheets, without any silks. A lot of time is needed to grow used to cleanliness, to the nakedness of things, to the absence of adornments, to the raw truth.

So our son has gone back to our neighbor Moud. I know how difficult it is to live in that district, I know the dangers that lurk there, you would bring them up frequently, every day you'd urge me to move, but don't be afraid, my darling, it's a school like any other, poverty and street life, yes, and where else could he go? He won't die of hunger, that's certain, he'll live with kind hearts, that's certain too, my brother couldn't hold him back but he'll keep an eye on him from afar, he'll visit him often, and one day he'll bring him back to our campsites when he's ready, when he will have quenched his thirst for everyday difficulties and the dangers of the street. Maybe I'm saying this for myself, to reassure myself, to reassure you: you have always had a horror of misery.

■ ■ ■

Ah, how I'd like to tell you beautiful things, the way Ramla used to do, the old woman soothsayer where you frequently dragged me off to. We'd sit down on an old mat and wait, me skeptical, often quietly mocking, you silent and a little worried. Despite her already advanced age, Ramla had a queen's bearing and the look of a courtesan. She would lean forward, her chin on her hands, mutter incomprehensible words, then throw her cowrie shells that would roll down and scatter lightly, she'd be silent for a moment, question them with her gaze, raise her head, and then I'd hear your impatient breathing, and emerging from the very depths of mystery, in a muffled voice, Ramla would utter words that seemed to rise to the heavens, she'd point at the cowries and decode their position, the way they lay strewn, the way they were grouped. Her words were often prescient but always of happy events, always moments of delight, that's why you'd pick up those cowries that heralded bliss and you kissed them, and grew radiant: you had drunk at the source, you had quenched your thirst for beautiful promises. Who can blame you for believing in good omens? Life is full of tellers of fortune, they create books, they write articles, they talk on television, in parliaments, they wage war as well, and you, you'd only listen to a music that would caress your spirit, there's no harm in that.

In prison, you see, I've lost the logic that used to sustain me a bit, I've vomited words that came to my tongue spontaneously and that I called reflections, I've freed myself from the pincers of the mind that kept me trapped, I don't believe in mathematics anymore, I now believe in oases that can spring up for no reason in the middle of harsh droughts, and what you taught me is that the best reason in the world lies dormant inside us, that it wakes up when it wants to and doesn't need any soliloquies to exist. You were so quick to grasp the word, the expression of daily life, you didn't need my 'nonsense' to fit in with things.

You knew so well how to induce pipe dreams, lower the barrier of common sense, let your desires speak out. When I lied to you, when I kept insisting that I was rich, that a fortune was coming my way, and that all we needed was to wait a little until my brother came back and the entire part of my inheritance would be handed over to me, you would look at me without saying a word, you would clutch the rope of the dream I was holding out to you.

I know that my phrases were often shaky, my words became uncertain, it hurt me more and more to be telling lies, making promises that weren't going to be kept, and you, too, felt the cracks in my voice, you began to suspect the lies, but you weren't ready yet to accept the void, the immense hole that the truth would dig, you were afraid of the disillusions and the somber prospects that would be the result, oh yes, we were both wearing a blindfold over our eyes, we'd hug each other so we wouldn't grope in the dark, so we wouldn't head straight for the abyss.

There's an immense uproar at the other end of the prison....

THE SON

One day I decided I would go to kiss my sister Malika, I would play with her and whisper: 'Weni, I love you', and my uncle-my-mother's-brother could just go fly a kite if he wanted. I left, I was running fast, I was in a hurry, I had a lump in my throat, the house wasn't locked and like an idiot I went in, I didn't ask, I wasn't even scared anymore, and I saw Malika sitting on a potty, peeing in the court-yard, and I hugged her, just like that on the potty, she cried and I mumbled: 'It's me, your brother, don't you recognize me?' She kept crying and I was yelling at her: 'I'm your brother, I'm your brother', and then Mouna, the wife of my uncle-my-mother's-brother came from her bedroom and started to cry, too, she took me in her arms: 'Go before your uncle comes home!' I answered: 'I just want to kiss my little sister!' 'That's fine, but your uncle doesn't like that, I'll talk to him later, now go!' I wasn't listening to her, I kept telling Malika: 'I'm your big brother, don't you recognize me?' and Malika was still crying and I was still kissing her, on her cheek, on her head, and then I left running, because I didn't want to cry in front of the wife of my uncle.

That very evening, my uncle came to the house, I hid, only mother Maria and the children were there, and he was screaming: 'Why did that bastard, that assassin's son, come to my house, why did he come? As far as I'm concerned, the little girl is not his sister, she's just my sister's daughter, he is the son of his bastard of a father, he's not to come into my house, he's not to speak to the people in my house, or else I'll kill him, I'll slit his throat and I'll slit his assassin father's throat right inside his prison.' Mother Maria said nothing but: 'Easy! Easy!' And he kept on screaming and making gestures. Then, just as he was leaving, father Moud arrived, and he was angry: 'Get out of my house, you fool, you infidel, get out, have you no shame!' My uncle yelled, 'Shame on you yourself, having this criminal's son in your house!' Father Moud responded, 'Infidel, it's your sister's son!' 'No, it's his father's son. Look at him!' And father Moud pushed him out: 'If you ever come back here again, I'll break your face!' My uncle-my-mother's-brother left, swinging his arms and grumbling darkly.

Mama really didn't like the neighborhood, PK7, she'd say it made no sense, it's all poor folks, ignorant and unimportant people, it's dirty, it's nasty, there are too many thieves, too many without a job, it's no good for the children. Nice people, she'd say, live in nice neighborhoods, like our cousins. But I didn't like going to see them, our cousins, their children had clean clothes but they didn't know anything, they watched television, that's all, they didn't even know how to play, and they were wusses, even when I'd fight with them just a little, they'd call their mother, that's all they did, they wouldn't raise a hand to me, and when I'd say anything, they just kept repeating: 'You can't say that, you can't say that', they didn't even know how to talk. My cousin Fadel was always clean and his hair was neat, and he had a room all to himself, and there were plenty of toys in his room, but he didn't know how to do anything, he'd say to me: 'You're poor!' and I'd answer: 'I'll do to your mother what you're thinking of!' and he'd go: 'You can't say that.' I would insult him; 'Shut up!' And I'd push him, he wouldn't react, he was a wuss, he'd just cry. When Mama would take me there, I didn't like to stay, I'd ask her every minute: 'Are we going home yet?' and she'd ask me to wait, she liked to talk to our cousin, she wanted to stay longer but in the end I'd cry, so then she would really scold me badly: 'You're just like your father, you like disgusting things!' Too bad.

The kids from the Beyda district, from the Clinique crossroads, came to the Play one time, there were lots of them, at least ten, and they were tough, almost grown-ups. We, Momo's team, we weren't there, we were all at the beach, only Sidi was there, the muezzin's son, they beat him up really badly, they broke one of his teeth, then they pissed on him and nobody said anything, even Django the proprietor was afraid because they had knives. They were threatening: 'We'll get the PK7 kids and their sisters and their mothers.' They left because of the cops; and afterwards, I swear, true is true, we were scared, we didn't say a thing but we were scared, even Momo wasn't feeling all that great. 'We'll piss on them, those bastards', he bragged, but we wouldn't, we knew it. Sidi's parents went to the police to lodge a complaint against the PK8 kids, the police came but Django, the proprietor, stated: 'It's not the PK8 kids', and the people there added: 'It's the kids from Beyda.' The police know the Beyda kids and one cop even said: 'Luckily, they didn't kill him.' The Beyda kids didn't come back, we forgot about them and those bastards from PK8 keep saying that we were shaking in our boots and wetting our pants. It's not true.

One day, the police caught me and even put me in their pen. I thought I would die, but I got out quickly, I'm telling you.

There was nothing at the house that day, and when I say nothing, I mean nothing, not even any cakes. Mother Maria was in bed, she had a headache, she was throwing up all the time, and she was nauseated, too. Father Moud hadn't been home in two days, the children were crying and Momo hadn't found anything outside either. So he asked me to follow him: 'You see, the new merchant, after the shop of Meimoune-who-sells-anything, after that of one-eyed Dahi, he's old, he can't see well, you go in there, then ask for Omo soap, it's high up on a shelf in his shop, he'll get a ladder and while he climbs up you open the drawer, you take the money and run, he can't see anything, he won't recognize you, afterwards he'll shout: 'A young thief!' That's all. Can you do it? You're not afraid? It's for Selma and Toto, they're crying all the time. 'I said, 'No, I'm not afraid', and I took off.

The old man was small and skinny and his eyes kept blinking. Me, I forgot the name Omo; I looked up and saw large boxes, I pointed at them, he took the ladder and went up, and, presto, I turned around and opened the drawer. When he saw me, he yelled, but his voice wasn't very loud and he couldn't jump off; I took some bills and ran but his son was just coming home and saw me. 'No problem', I thought, 'he's new, he doesn't even know me!' But yes, he did know me, the bastard, and the police came to the house to pick me up. Momo really tried: 'He didn't go out!' Mother Maria, who knew nothing about it, said: 'He didn't do it', but the cop whacked me. 'Into the car, you thug!' I didn't even cry, I wanted to, but Momo was there, and Mokhis and Édenté and Papis, so I didn't cry. At the police station they frisked me, they called me a son of a bitch, a bastard's bastard, then they locked me up in a dark cell; when the door slammed shut my stomach hurt; at first I couldn't see anything, but then I noticed a kid from Beyda who was sleeping, he had those signs on his arms they burn into their skin with matches, he was fast asleep; those Beyda kids don't care, they're always in prison; there was a very stocky man, too, without a shirt, he was looking at me without saying anything, I was really scared and I was crying, crying very softly. Then the man comforted me: 'It's nothing, little man, it's nothing, you'll get out, your father will come, and your mother', but I didn't say where my father and my mother were, I was just crying very softly, the man gave me a piece of chewing gum, I was really hungry, I don't know where it came from but I took it, then he muttered some things I didn't understand and he asked: 'Isn't that so?' I answered: 'Yes, it is', and then the kid from Beyda woke up: 'You're one of those PK7 bastards, aren't you?' I didn't answer, he got up but the man told him to sit down and then he left me alone. After that I didn't speak, I just stayed inside my head. Now I'm like Papa, I'm in prison and I've done nothing wrong, I swear that I'd forgotten about the old man's shop. I was hot so I took off my shirt and said to myself: father Moud will come and he'll start yelling on the square in front and he'll say: 'It's you who are the thieves, not us, the poor people...' and so on, and then they'll let me go. Father Moud didn't come. But I did hear a noise and a cop opened the cell door and called me in a nice voice: 'Come, young one!' The old shop-keeper and his son were there and the old man said: 'It wasn't him!' and the kid was shaking: 'It wasn't him, I made a mistake, it wasn't him, I saw the real one afterwards, but I don't know his name.' I didn't understand what was going on, the cop swore at him very loudly, and took down my name. 'Get out of here!' I ran home, Momo and the others were waiting for me, they carried me, treated me like a brave man but I didn't get it. Later they explained to me, they'd gotten hold of the kid, the shopkeeper's son, and showed him their knives: 'You get going, you tell your father that it wasn't him, then you tell the same thing to the police, or else we'll come back tonight to cut your throat, so get going and say: "I saw the real guy, this isn't him", and you say nothing else to anyone, not even to your father, right?' The kid agreed, he was afraid and he wanted to be our friend, so he did what they told him to do. And the old shopkeeper even came to the house that night and apologized to mother Maria. 'My son is an idiot, he didn't see him very well, he's nearsighted; but then he understood, he admitted it, he's not a bad boy', and the old man even left a few coins for mother Maria to help her get medical care. But mother Maria never goes to the hospital for herself, never; she takes care of herself or with the marabou's help, he gives her white sand that she puts on her head, that's all.

Once, in front of the prison, I was sitting under the tree, watching the big gate, then I started thinking, I was thinking that nothing was nice anymore: Momo would leave for the garage every day, at night he was tired, he'd get dressed really nice and go, he no longer took me along, and Mokhis was too evil, and Sara would now pass by very quickly and not say anything, just 'hello', then she'd keep going. My uncle-my-mother's-brother was really evil, too, and I didn't see Malika anymore. The kids didn't play much anymore, they were stealing too much, and even I didn't feel like playing any longer. And Papa wasn't coming out of prison, and I still didn't know where Mama's grave was. I was living inside my thoughts, I didn't see the guard right beside me, I was scared. 'I didn't do anything' I said, but he grabbed my hand and took me away. 'Come!' I didn't cry but my stomach was rumbling, I pulled my hand back a little and said again: 'Leave me alone, I didn't do anything!' not too loudly so he wouldn't get mad, but the guard brought me to the big gate, he said something and they opened a small door in the big gate and we went inside, I was very scared now. There were a lot of people behind huge bars, and then we went to a room with a table and chairs and he told me to sit down. Well, I cried, it's true, I'm not hiding anything from you. 'Don't cry, just tell me why you're always coming here.' 'It's for Papa.' He asked me for Papa's name, he went away and came back with him, I swear, Papa had a big beard and he was very skinny, and he had tears in his eyes, and he kissed me over and over again.

'Are you in good health?'

I said yes.

'Do you see Malika?'

I said yes.

'She's in good health?'

I said yes.

'Why aren't you with your uncle, my brother?'

I didn't say anything.

'Why aren't you at school?'

I didn't say anything.

'Didn't I ask you not to come here anymore?'

I didn't say anything.

'How's my friend, the one with whom you live?'

'He's fine.'

'He's a good man.'

'Very good!'

'Why are you crying? Men don't cry.'

I didn't say anything.

'You mustn't cry anymore, you mustn't come here anymore. You must study, then work, be a man, you must only think about yourself and about your sister.'

'Will you come out, Papa?'

'One day, maybe, when you're grown.'

'I'll wait.'

'No, you mustn't come here anymore, swear it!'

'I did already.'

'Swear it again!'

I didn't.

So then Papa got angry, he grabbed my shoulders and looked at me hard and asked me again: 'Swear it!' there was water in his eyes and I was trembling and I didn't want to cry again, he shook me, so I swore, then he let me go, and he kissed me for a long time:

'Now you've got to go. Don't forget about your sister, don't forget that I love you both very much.'

So I left and just before I went out the door, he called me:

'You know that I loved your mother very much?'

I told him I knew and I left very quickly so I wouldn't cry again.

That night it was cold, very cold, there was no blanket, only for the little ones and for mother Maria, me, Momo and father Moud, we had nothing, that's how it is, men leave things for others. Momo and me, we picked up the small, very thin and very dirty mattresses we had in the house and put those over our body, at first it smelled of I don't know what, but then it gave us a bit of warmth and we could sleep. I thought about my cousin Fadel who has plenty of clothes, blankets, a bike, television and his father and his mother and his little sister, and then I told myself: 'He's in his room, he has everything, if I were him it would be fine, oh, I'd be just fine', but then I thought: 'No, I wouldn't be playing with the PK7 kids anymore, Momo wouldn't be my friend, Papa wouldn't be my Papa and Mama wouldn't be my Mama and Malika would be someone else's little sister, no, I don't want to be anybody else', and I almost cried, I swear, I didn't want to be anybody else.

Mother Maria's cakes aren't selling much anymore, we just eat the leftovers. She's done everything, but the cakes don't sell anymore, even the marabout came, he spat and all that, but it didn't work. Mother Maria was tired, she was working hard, she didn't even hit the children anymore when they were screaming and she didn't pick up her baby when he was crying, all she did was busy herself with the cakes, but one day father Moud said: 'It's not worth the trouble now that you can find them in the grocery stores, where they're packaged and sold, they leave nothing for the poor any longer.'

You can see mother Maria, small, thin like this and with her old veil, all black, all worn out, you think she's nothing, but no, she's very strong, she started to make couscous and that works, not like her cakes, but still she sells it, and ever since then we're eating couscous, there's not always meat in it, but that's alright, we put powdered milk on it. Toto doesn't yell, Selma says nothing, and Tenn, he'll eat no matter what, and me, I'm fine, it's very good, it's just Momo who doesn't eat this anymore, for him it's whatever, he buys sandwiches at the Lebanese, mother Maria thinks it's for pigs and it's too expensive, but I'm thrilled when he gives me some.

I saw Sara once, she was waiting for the bus, I stared at her so she'd call me, but she wasn't looking at me, so I walked right past her, threw down my marbles so she'd see me and then I picked them up again, but Sara didn't call me. Then Momo got off the bus and stopped to talk with Sara. He stayed to wait with Sara for another bus, it gave me a headache, I didn't understand it at all, why was Sara not seeing me, why wasn't she taking the bus, why was she talking with Momo for such a long time? I felt sick and I was mad with Momo that night, I couldn't say why.

One day there was more political stuff, not the political stuff of before, but big politics to choose the president, with the photos of those who want to be president. Well, it's the President-on-the-photograph who will remain president, of course, but people are still going to vote no matter what. Anyhow, for us it's always good. Because we, we find lots of money, we set up tents on the streets with the women, we put the President-on-the-photograph all over the place, we haul stuff around, we scream, we paste, we rip off, it's great. Mother Maria put a tent in front of the house and placed a big photo of the President-on-the-photograph, a customer at the market who always buys her couscous brought the tent, and the photos and even a cassette with music for the President-on-the-photograph, and she gave some more money to mother Maria, who was very happy. The customer even forgot her couscous. Selma and Toto are dancing in the little tent, and at night me and Momo sleep in it, it's better than the court-yard and we stand guard, too, and mother Maria's customer will give us coins for that, it's all good.

Us kids, we go into town, there are tents everywhere, and music, and cars honking their horns, and we find forgotten things, and then we take some stuff, too, especially from women's bags. Only, when father Moud came home and saw the tent and the photos, he yelled:

'What's all this? Take it down!' but mother Maria negotiated with him and he dropped it. 'In any case, they're all the same, all corrupt.' That's how he is, father Moud.

Momo now says things like: 'Shouldn't steal anymore', and also: 'When you take something you won't go to paradise', and also: 'The PK7 kids are all crooks'. He talks trash, Momo, I just listen quietly. I don't know why he talks like that, Momo, but I finally got it, he's talking like Sara, he repeats the same things that Sara says. At the same time, Momo does what he always did, he steals parts from the garage, I know he does. It's normal. But why does he talk that way?

One day, my uncle-my-mother's-brother left with his whole family, even my sister Malika, he took her away, the house was empty, nobody there at all, from the distance all I saw was the open door, I watched it for a long time, I went over very carefully, and there was nobody, nobody, I even went in very carefully. I called: 'Malika! Malika!', nobody, so I almost cried, I called again, nothing; a neighbor came out, I asked: 'Did they leave?' 'Yesterday, during the night, they told no one.' So I felt like someone had hit me over the head and I went to see Meimoune-who-sells-anything: 'Excuse me, Meimoune, tell me where he is now, my uncle-my-mother's brother?' 'Why are you asking about him, he doesn't even recognize you?', I didn't answer. Then he said: 'He's been saying for a long time that PK7 is for losers, that the people here are morons, that they say bad things about his sister and that they take your father's side, all of them, and that you, he doesn't want to see you anymore, and not your father's friends either. He left during the night, without a word, he thinks he's a boss now because he got a promotion, I don't even know where he is, he didn't even pay me.'

I went to the cemetery and I told Mama, from a distance, that everything was fine, that Malika was fine and me too, that I was going to school and that I wasn't a crook and that Papa was going to get out and that soon, tomorrow, we'd all be together in our house. Then again, no, you shouldn't tell lies. Maybe, in her grave, Mama knows everything. Suddenly I started up again: 'PK7 is over with, Malika isn't there anymore, she left with your brother, why doesn't he like me? And then, too, Papa asked me not to come see him anymore, and now Momo, I don't know anymore… Mama, there are a lot of things I don't understand anymore, but all that's only today, Mama, Meimoune-who-sells-anything, he says: 'One day it goes your way, one day it goes against you', tomorrow me, I'll be grown, soon, I swear to you, and I'll be a policeman, and I'll set Papa free and I'll go get Malika and I'll go to our house and we'll be fine, we'll hang your photo on the wall, the beautiful photo of your wedding with Papa, you remember, you were beautiful… and then, and that's all, Mama, we'll make you a beautiful grave also, I swear, Mama, everything will be fine…'

At the house I slept a little, I was tired and then Momo came, he ate, he washed up, he left, and when I woke up Selma had received a coin and Toto also and they told me: 'Momo gave it to us, but you were sleeping', so I left to look for Momo. I looked for him at Mokhis' house, he wasn't there, then in a tiny street I saw it: Sara standing up against the wall and, I swear, Momo kissing her on the mouth, it was a bit dark, but I saw it all, even when he told Sara very softly: 'I love you' and stuff like that, I swear to you, they didn't even notice me, so I took off very fast, I went back to the house telling myself: 'You shouldn't cry, you shouldn't cry', but it all hurt, here, inside, and to tell the truth, I was crying very softly, and I went to bed. Later Momo came home and spoke to mother Maria, he kissed Selma and Toto, he saw that I was in bed, he put a coin next to me, under the old pillow. Me, I threw it far away and screamed: 'I don't want your money, you creep!' He put the coin back in his pocket, then I heard him say: 'He's a fool, that kid!' he laughed, he asked mother Maria: 'What's his problem?' 'I don't know. Did you do anything to him?' He answered: 'No, maybe it's because I didn't take him along to the garage. I'll take him tomorrow!' Me, I almost said: 'I don't give a fuck about your garage, or about you and Sara!' But I kept quiet, I pretended to be asleep and then I slept.

I didn't feel good for several days, I didn't go out and I didn't do anything and I didn't speak to Momo or Selma or Toto, not even to Tenn, I didn't laugh at the faces he made and I helped mother Maria with her couscous, that's all I did. Father Moud didn't even come home anymore and she wasn't very happy, so I stayed with her to help with her couscous and her cakes, she was still making some of those, and she said: 'Of all the children you're the best,' but me, I didn't answer. And then my uncle-my-father's-brother came back, I didn't run away, he kissed me, he gave me presents, then he went to see mother Maria, he sat down with her, they talked for a long time, he got up, he kissed me again, he went out, he didn't say: 'Come!' but I followed him. He stopped and asked me: 'Is there something you want?' I said: 'I'm leaving with you', and he was happy, very happy, I can assure you, and he went to tell mother Maria, she kissed me, then she gave me some cakes, and she cried, too. That's how I left the PK7 and everyone down there.

Now, I'm still thinking about all that, I swear, and it's very strong, I tell you, it's too strong because I really love those people there, yes, I love my Mama and also my Papa and then Sara and I even still love Momo, and father Moud and mother Maria of course, and I love my sister Malika a lot, and Tenn, and Toto, and Selma, and even all the kids of PK7, I love them all, I think of them, and it hurts, I swear to you, because it's not good to love people so much, it makes your stomach hurt when they're far away, or when there's something wrong with them, and it just makes you too unhappy, and then you know, it's just too hard, because me, now, every time, I feel like crying and that's no good, I have to be a man, don't I?

TRANSLATOR'S
ACKNOWLEDGMENTS

For this beautiful edition my most sincere gratitude goes first of all to Evan Johnston who has proven that 'a picture can, indeed, be worth a thousand words'. Thank you for making this such a lovely *looking* book.

Warm thanks, as always, to Tim Schaffner who never ceases to inspire me with respect and admiration for the titles he chooses to publish. It is an ongoing privilege for me to be one of the translators on his remarkable list of books.

A heartfelt thank you to Alice Tassel of the French Publishers' Agency for encouraging works like this to be translated and published.

And, last but never least, my enduring gratitude to David Vita, my husband, for always being my exceptionally valuable and supportive first reader.

—MDJ

AUTHOR BIOGRAPHY

MBAREK OULD BEYROUK (BEYROUK) is a French-speaking Mauritanian writer (1957–). A journalist and author of three novels and a collection of short stories, he received the Ahmadou-Kourouma prize for his novel *Le Tambour des Larmes* (The Drum of Tears) in 2016, as well as the Prix du roman métis des lycéens .

Beyrouk studied law at the University of Rabat but turned to journalism. After working for the official media, in 1988 he founded the country's first independent newspaper, "Mauritanie Demain". He then became a member of the High Authority for the Press and Audiovisual, created in 2006.In 2016, he was appointed adviser to the presidency of the republic by former Mauritanian president Mohamed Ould Abdelaziz.

He is the author of the novels, *And the sky forgot to rain*, 2006, *Desert News*, 2009 , *The Emir's Griot*, 2013 , *The Drum of Tears*, 2015, and *I am alone*, 2018. *Parias*, 2021 , Sabine Wespieser Editions, is the first complete work of his to be translated and published in the United States.

TRANSLATOR BIOGRAPHY

MARJOLIJN DE JAGER Born in Indonesia (1936), raised in The Netherlands, and residing in the USA since the age of 22, Marjolijn de Jager earned a PhD. in Romance Languages and Literatures from UNC-Chapel Hill in 1975. She translates from both the Dutch and the French, with a special love of Francophone African literature, particularly women's voices. Among her honors are an NEA grant, two NEH grants and, in 2011, the annually awarded ALA Distinguished Member Award from the African Literature Association for scholarship, teaching, and translations of African Literature. In 2021, her translation of *The Mediterranean Wall* by Louis-Philippe Dalembert, (Schaffner Press) won the French Voices Grand Prize for Best Translated Book. She has to date translated five titles for Schaffner Press,with her latest, *Milwaukee Blues* by Louis-Philippe Dalembert to be released in May of 2023.For further information please see http://mdejager.com